**Robyn Anderson**

Robyn is spunky and very tall for her age—which is eleven. She likes her dark-brown hair to be kept short. She has brown eyes and tans easily in the Michigan sun. Competitive, smart and fun, Robyn enjoys being part of any adventure.

**Nick Tysman**

One phrase best describes ten-year-old Nick, and that is "easy going." He likes being outdoors, playing in sports and backpacking with his family out West. His brown hair and brown eyes make him look like he could almost be Johnnie's younger brother.

**Joey Thomas**

Joey's light brown hair and hazel green eyes, coupled with his round face, make him look angelic. Openly curious about everything, Joey likes hanging out with the other Gun Lake kids. Like Katy, Joey is nine years old and attends Chief Noonday Elementary School.

**Travis Hughes**

Travis—the picture of the perfect athlete. His sandy-blond hair, blue eyes and tanned skin make him popular with the girls. When Johnnie came into town, Travis wasn't too sure he could "hang" with someone who used a wheelchair. He and Johnnie are friends—but not close.

# Acknowledgments

The inspiration for this book came from a visit to Eagle Mount in Billings, Montana that Johnnie took a few years ago. Eagle Mount is a place where, despite ability or disability, anyone can join in the adventure of life if he or she is willing to adapt. For more information about their program, you can visit their website:
www.eaglemountbillings.org.

Special acknowledgment goes to Sharon's son Joshua Lamson for his insightful contributions to the adventure scenes. Raised on adventure books as a small boy, he helped shape the challenges that Johnnie, Danny, Robyn and Katy encountered in this book.

# Table of Contents

CHAPTER 1

# Christmas Surprise

"I'll take good care of Steamer for you while you're gone," Nick said, as he took the house key Johnnie held out for him. "I wish I were going with you, but my grandparents are coming to our house for Christmas this year."

"Yeah, I wish you were coming too," Johnnie said. "But I'm sure glad you can watch my dog for me. And if it makes you feel any better, remember that Joey and Travis aren't coming along either."

"Well, Joey is heading off to his grandparents' house in Wisconsin, and Travis gets to go to Florida," Nick complained. "Besides, you'll have Danny, Katy and Robyn with you."

Johnnie shifted in his wheelchair as he stared at the ground. He said, "I promise to bring you back something really *suh-weet* from Montana." His eyes drifted up to his friend's face.

Nick grinned. "Maybe a real bear's tooth from the Bear Tooth Mountains?"

Johnnie laughed. "Only if it's already on the ground. I don't want to play dentist with some grizzly."

Nick fingered the key Johnnie had given him. "I really hope you have a great time," he said. "If you guys have any adventures, be sure to tell me *everything!* I want details!"

Johnnie started to wheel himself down the sidewalk to where his father waited for him in the van. He turned and said, "My biggest adventure is going to be skiing down the mountainside!"

Nick grinned and waved goodbye to his friend.

\* \* \*

That night Johnnie snuggled beneath the comforter on his bed. He stared at the ceiling, dimly lit by the nightlight in his room. "We're getting on an airplane and flying to Billings, Montana tomorrow morning," he whispered to himself. "What a great Christmas this is going to be."

He turned on his side and looked at his suitcase,

packed and ready to load into the van. He didn't have to pack any ski gear, as Red Lodge Mountain, where their winter adventure would begin, had plenty of rental equipment. Red Lodge Mountain used to be called Grizzly Peak. Johnnie liked that name better. "It's more scary," he had told his parents.

"Scary?" his father had exclaimed. "Now don't start thinking that you and your friends are going to solve any high-mountain mysteries. This is a family vacation and we're all going to stick together and have fun!"

Johnnie chuckled as he remembered that conversation. Already he and Danny had done an Internet search on ghost towns around Billings. They planned to talk their parents into visiting one sometime during their ten-day stay.

Johnnie closed his eyes and recalled the day his parents, along with the Randalls and Andersons, had asked all the kids out to dinner. It was shortly before Thanksgiving. At the restaurant, Mr. Jacobson, Johnnie's dad, pulled out a large box wrapped in Christmas paper and decorated with ribbon. Johnnie and his two sisters grabbed the box.

"Hey! This gift is for Danny, Katy and Robyn too,"

Mrs. Jacobson said.

Together the six kids tore open the paper and opened the box. Inside was a video tape labeled, "Eagle Mount Billings: On the Wings of Eagles."

"Uh, is this supposed to mean something?" Katy asked.

"Let's go back to our house for dessert, pop in the video and find out," Johnnie's dad said.

That evening Johnnie discovered that Eagle Mount, a recreational program, was started in 1984 for people with physical and developmental disabilities. Johnnie learned that even people with cerebral palsy—like he had—could enjoy all sorts of winter sports. Eagle Mount's original program began in Bozeman, Montana. Then two other Montana programs opened: one in Billings and the other in Great Falls.

Eagle Mount had both summer and winter activities, and it was the winter part of the tape that captured Johnnie's attention. People with all sorts of disabilities actually skied down the snowy, steep mountainside. One girl, who had only one leg, twisted and turned her way expertly through a ski course. She was training to be in the Paralympics—an athletic event held two weeks after the Olympic Games, usually in the same city.

Another skier sat in a specially designed seat that was mounted onto a single ski. These were called monoskis. The one shown in the video had handles attached to back of the seat so the ski instructor could guide the ski down the mountainside from behind.

The skier used outriggers to help balance himself on the slopes. The outriggers were poles with little flexible skis attached. The cuffs at the top of the outrigger fit around the skier's arms.

Though Johnnie had lived in California all his life before moving to Michigan, the only skiing he had done was on the water. Carving a turn down a mountainside was going to be a whole new experience.

CHAPTER 2

# The Bear Tooth Mountains

"Will somebody *please* answer that phone?" Johnnie yelled as he buried his head under the pillow. The ringing continued, long and relentless.

"Hey! Wait a minute! That's no telephone. That's my alarm clock," Johnnie cried. He threw his pillow onto the floor, grabbed the clock and hit the off button. "Six thirty!"

He stretched, rubbed his eyes and transferred into his wheelchair. "Time for a shower," he said. "Then off into the wild blue yonder!"

A half hour later, Johnnie rolled himself into the kitchen. A bowl of cereal and some juice awaited him at the table. His parents were busily going over their checklist.

Johnnie's older sisters Corry and Elsa joined Johnnie

at the breakfast table. "I hope there are some cute guys at the lodge," Corry said.

"Me too!" Elsa agreed.

Johnnie rolled his eyes. "This is a ski trip, not a let's-check-out-the-cute-guys trip."

"Hey! You have *your* kind of fun, and we'll have ours," Corry replied. She finished the last spoonful of cereal and headed for her room. "Gotta finish packing," she called back.

Elsa took all the breakfast dishes to the sink. "Don't worry, Johnnie," she said as she rinsed and put them in the dishwasher. "We'll have plenty of time to ski with you and your friends."

"Okay, everybody," Johnnie's father interrupted. "It's almost seven-thirty. We've got just a half hour to pack up everything and leave. We need to be at the airport no later than nine o'clock."

"Why so early?" Johnnie asked. "Our plane doesn't leave until noon."

"When we made the plane reservations and told them you were traveling with your wheelchair, the agent told us to be at the gate at least two hours before departure time," Mr. Jacobson answered. "We'll check our bags, but we can easily take apart your wheelchair and store it in the plane's baggage closet."

"Will we get to board the plane before everyone else?" Johnnie asked.

"Yes," came the reply.

"But what about the Randalls and the Andersons?"

"Johnnie, don't worry about it. When we made the reservations, we had our seat assignments loaded into the computer. We're going to sit in the bulkhead—you know, the first row of seats in business class, and the others will sit nearby. We will all get to Montana on the same plane at the same time."

Satisfied, Johnnie headed to his room to stuff a few more items into his backpack. He fought off the urge to call Danny and find out how soon they'd be leaving for the airport. "We'll all get to Montana at the same time," he reminded himself.

\* \* \*

At the airport, the family checked their baggage at the ticket counter. Johnnie and his sisters carried backpacks with them stuffed with books, cameras,  and other things they thought were absolutely essential. After clearing the security checkpoint where their backpacks were scanned and opened, they headed toward the gate.

"Can I have the window seat?" Johnnie asked his dad.

"Sure!" Mr. Jacobson answered.

Soon, Johnnie heard the gate attendant announce, "All passengers requiring assistance please prepare to board. Have your boarding passes ready."

"That's us," Mr. Jacobson said to Johnnie. "Your mother and sisters will board in just a few minutes."

Johnnie wheeled himself to the boarding checkpoint where a flight attendant met him.

"Hi! My name is Doug," the attendant said. "I'll take you to your seat."

Doug wheeled Johnnie through the jetway to the plane's entrance, while Mr. Jacobson followed. They stopped at the door to the plane, and Mr. Jacobson helped Johnnie transfer from his wheelchair to a specially built aisle chair the airline owned. It was narrow enough to be wheeled down the airplane's aisles to his seat.  "Just a quick trip to first-class," Doug said with a smile.

"Whoa! First class? How cool is that?" Johnnie looked at the wide, comfortable seats.

"If you need any assistance during the flight, let me know," Doug said. He smiled and left.

Meanwhile, Mr. Jacobson disassembled Johnnie's wheelchair and helped another attendant load it into the baggage closet. Then he took his seat beside Johnnie. A few minutes later, Mrs. Jacobson walked past them on their way to the business-coach section. "I get the first-class seat on the way back," Mrs. Jacobson quickly whispered to her husband.

Johnnie adjusted the air conditioning  vents located above him, and then he took out a book from his backpack and began to read. About fifteen minutes later, he looked up and saw Robyn walk down the aisle, closely followed by her parents.

"Hey!" she said, when she saw Johnnie. "I'm sitting just two rows behind your mom, and I think Danny and Katy are sitting on the other side of us. Just think, in about five hours, we'll be landing in Montana!"

Not too long after, Johnnie looked up and saw his friend Danny.

"I'm sitting back there with my dad," he said. "I sure wish I could sit up here with you."

Mr. Jacobson smiled. "I'll tell you what. As soon as

we're in the air and the pilot has turned off the seatbelt sign, I'll ask the flight attendant if I can switch places with you."

"Cool!" Danny said, and headed back to his seat.

Johnnie watched people steadily stream into the plane. "I can't believe all these people are going to Montana," he said to his dad.

"Not all of them are," his father answered. "We're all going to Minneapolis, Minnesota. Some people will stay there and others, like ourselves, will board another plane and take off for some other city. Our group may be the only one from this plane to travel on to Montana."

After a few minutes, all the passengers were seated. The flight attendants walked down the aisles shutting the overhead bins and making sure everyone had fastened their seatbelts. Before long, Johnnie felt the plane begin to move. The attendants began to give their pre-flight instructions about exits and oxygen masks, as the plane turned onto the runway. Then all the attendants fastened themselves into their seats. Johnnie looked out the window and saw the scenery go by, faster and faster. Then before he knew it, he felt the plane lift off the ground. In just a matter of seconds, he was looking down at the airport and the streets of Grand Rapids, Michigan.

"Chew some gum or just swallow to unblock your ears," Johnnie's dad said.

"Wow!" Johnnie said. "This is the coolest thing we've *ever* done."

In just a few minutes, the plane had reached its cruising altitude, and the pilot turned off the seatbelt signs and said that people could "move about the cabin" if they wanted to. Mr. Jacobson spoke with the attendant about switching seats with Danny.

"That's fine, the attendant said. "But when we're getting ready to land, you'll have to switch back."

Mr. Jacobson slipped out of his seat and went back to explain everything to Danny. Soon, Danny and Johnnie were chatting and taking turns looking out the window.

\* \* \*

The flight to Minnesota was smooth and, after switching airplanes, the group was Montana bound. There wasn't much to see out the window except the tops of clouds, so Johnnie concentrated on the movie being shown. When the movie ended, Johnnie raised the window shade and gasped in surprise.

"Danny, look!"

Below them were snow-covered mountain peaks, dotted with a few trees. The plane gradually made its descent into Billings, Montana.

"We will be landing at the Billings airport in just a few minutes," the pilot announced. "The weather is sunny and thirty-five degrees."

"Thirty-five degrees!" Johnnie cried. "There won't be any snow!"

A fellow passenger leaned across the aisle and said, "Oh yes, there'll be plenty of snow. There's always snow in the mountains!"

\* \* \*

Once they landed, Johnnie retrieved his wheelchair and rolled himself through the wide airport walkways to the baggage claim area where they picked up their luggage. Then they headed to the car rental desk. Johnnie waited while his father secured the keys to the van that Mr. Jacobson had reserved for them. The Andersons and Randalls planned to share another van.

"Can Danny ride with us?" Johnnie asked his dad.

Mr. Jacobson smiled. "I guess that would be fine. With all these girls around, you two guys had better stick together!"

Soon the whole bunch of them—twelve people in all—headed southwest from the airport on their way to Red Lodge.

"These mountains remind me a lot of California," Johnnie remarked to Danny. "A couple of times we went sledding, but never skiing. This is going to be so cool."

As they drove closer to Red Lodge, Mrs. Jacobson pointed up ahead. "Look! According to the map, those are the Bear Tooth Mountains."

Johnnie leaned forward in the seat. Ahead of him were jagged snow-covered mountain peaks that did indeed look like a bear's lower jaw. He sat back in his seat.

"And I'll bet there's some wilderness adventures waiting for us," he whispered to Danny.

* * *

It was late afternoon before they arrived at the motel in Red Lodge. It took another hour to unload everything and get situated in their rooms. After a quick dinner at the motel's restaurant, they decided to check in at the ski lodge.

"We have classes that begin tomorrow morning,"

Gary Schmidt, one of the ski instructors, said. "This is one of the best beginner mountains in the country—especially our Lazy M run, which is two and a half miles long."

"How many trails are up here?" Danny asked.

"We have seventy trails, but not all of them are open all the time," Gary answered. "We also have eight lifts."

"How high up are we?" Robyn asked.

"Well, the highest elevation is about 9,400 feet. The base of the mountain, is about 7,000 feet higher than sea level. That gives you close to a 2,400-foot vertical drop—like skiing down two Empire State Buildings stacked on top of one another. Only, of course, our trails slope gradually instead of just dropping straight down."

Robyn's eyes grew wide, and Johnnie had to laugh. "Don't worry, Robyn, you're not going to fall off the mountain," he said.

"What I want to know," Mrs. Anderson said, "is how this place was discovered—it's so far away from everything."

"I believe I can answer that." Johnnie turned and saw a gray-haired man with wiry whiskers ambling toward them. "My name is Abraham Bakker—friends call me

Abe. Back in the late 1880s, when coal-fueled locomotives were popular, miners from Finland, Ireland, Scotland, Italy, Yugoslavia and the Scandinavian countries flocked to this area and settled here. The mountains are rich with coal and other minerals. In just fifteen years, the population grew from 1,100 to 5,000.

"Yup. The town grew fast until 1943. That's when an explosion at the Smith Mine near Bearcreek killed seventy-four men. It was the worst coal mine disaster in Montana's history. Wasn't long before all the mines shut down. Nothin' left now but the old buildings and mine shafts."

"Ghost towns!" Johnnie blurted.

Abe smiled, a twinkle in his grey-blue eyes. "You got that right, young man. Ghost towns!"

"How many people live here now?" Mr. Jacobson asked.

"Well, I'd say there's about two thousand who live up here," Abe answered. "But with folks like yourself coming here to ski in the winter and enjoy other outdoor activities in the warmer months, who knows? We might grow to five thousand again. Kinda hope we don't, though." Then he winked at Johnnie and added, "It's peaceful up here—'cept for them ghosts."

## CHAPTER 3

# On the Way to Red Lodge

The alarm clock buzzed at 6:30 Saturday morning, but Johnnie was already up and in the shower. Today he would learn how to ski.

He dressed quickly, sat in his wheelchair and flipped aimlessly through the local TV channels as he waited for his parents and sisters to finish getting ready. He glanced at the clock on the nightstand. The digital readout showed 7:15.

"Are you guys ready *yet?*" he yelled at his sisters, who were in the adjoining bathroom.

Finally they emerged, every hair in place and makeup applied perfectly. Mrs. Jacobson looked at them and smiled. Mr. Jacobson just shook his head and handed everyone their ski jackets.

"Let's go," he said. "I think the Andersons and

Randalls are already in the parking lot waiting for us."

"Looks like it snowed last night," Mrs. Randall noted, as Johnnie and his family approached. "But it sure is sunny now. You kids be sure to wear plenty of sun block, and put on your sunglasses."

"In the restaurant?" Katy teased.

The rustic-looking restaurant was just a few blocks away but the walkways hadn't been cleared yet, making pushing a wheelchair very difficult. So the three families filed into the vans and drove the short distance. Delicious smells drifted past Johnnie's nose. His stomach growled in anticipation of being fed.

After a hearty breakfast of eggs, sausage, pancakes and hash brown potatoes, the group climbed back into the vans and headed for the resort. A fine powdery snow decorated the tall ponderosa pine trees, and the bright sunlight made them glitter against the blue sky.

"Look!" Elsa called out, as she pointed toward the forest.

Johnnie leaned forward to peer out the van's side window. He saw a quick flicker of white, then more movement.

"Deer!" he said.

"Those are white-tailed deer," Corry informed them.

"And how do you know that?" Elsa asked.

"When I found out we were going to Montana, I pulled some information off the Internet. Actually, we have whitetails in Michigan too. When there's danger, they raise their white tail like a flag as they run away."

"What other kinds of animals are here in Montana?" Johnnie asked.

"Well, of course there are grizzly bears. According to the article I read, there are only about 1,000 grizzly bears that live in the United States—not counting Alaska. And 800 of them live in Montana."

"Do they live around here?" Mrs. Jacobson asked, as she pulled her jacket tighter around her and craned her neck to see as far up into the mountains as she could.

"Well, there are probably some. Most of them live in Glacier Park, but a few live in Yellowstone, which isn't too far from here. But don't worry, they're hibernating now."

Mrs. Jacobson sighed and leaned back in her seat.

"But," Corry continued, "there are mountain lions and lynx too, and they *don't* hibernate."

Johnnie chuckled to himself when he saw his mother

suddenly sit up straighter and glance out the side window again.

"I've heard of mountain lions," Elsa said. "But what is a lynx?"

"I guess they're similar to a bobcat," Corry said. "According to the information I retrieved, the lynx are mostly nighttime hunters. And Montana has the most number of lynx in the continental United States."

"Continental?" Johnnie said.

"That means the lower forty-eight states," Mr. Jacobson interjected. "So it would exclude Alaska and Hawaii.

"There are also less threatening animals, like elk and moose," he continued, as he patted his wife's shoulder.

"And mountain goats," Johnnie said, picking up on his father's subtle hint to move the conversation from flesh-eating animals to herbivores—animals that eat plants.

"Probably the most fierce animals we're going to see today are the skiers," Mr. Jacobson joked.

## CHAPTER 4

# Down the Mountainside

At the ski lodge, Johnnie opened the van door and breathed in the crisp mountain air. He detected a hint of pine. He put on his sunglasses, because the glare of the sun off the snow-covered slopes was nearly blinding.

Just then he heard a familiar voice. "Welcome to Red Lodge! It's a perfect day to learn how to ski!" Johnnie looked up and saw the smiling face of Gary Schmidt, the ski instructor he had met the day before.

"Well, Johnnie," he said. "Are you ready to carve some curves and try a few jumps?"

Mrs. Jacobson gasped. "Jumps?"

Gary laughed. "Just kidding. While Johnnie here looks like he would be willing to try, we're going to take it nice and easy until he gets the hang of it."

Johnnie smiled as he saw his mother breathe a heavy

sigh of relief. Then Gary leaned down and whispered, "Later on, we'll get *adventurous!*" Gary's eyes sparkled with amusement.

The Randalls and Andersons headed toward the lodge to rent their gear. Gary told the Jacobsons to get fitted for whatever they needed. "I'll take care of Johnnie," he added.

At the lodge, Gary showed Johnnie the latest mono-ski they had. It was a Yetti. Basically it looked like a seat strapped onto a snow ski. Gary helped Johnnie transfer into the ski's seat. "This seat is positioned over cord center, which will place most of your weight on the tip of the ski," Gary explained. "This will help make turning easier. However, we can adjust the seat position to whatever feels best for you, once you've taken a few runs down the hill. The seat is attached to a special shock. When an able-bodied person skis, his legs—and mostly his knees—absorb all the bumps and turns along the way. But in a monoski, the shock takes the bumps, which means you won't get as tired as your friends over there!" Gary pointed to where Danny, Katy and Robyn were heading to the first ski lift.

Next, Gary handed Johnnie two poles that had cuffs

at one end and little moveable skis on the bottom. "These are outriggers," Gary explained. "They'll help you maintain your balance, especially in the turns. You'll control the ski using your upper body—much like you do when you water ski."

"How'd you know I water ski?" Johnnie asked.

"It's amazing what I know," Gary answered. He smiled then said, "Okay, I admit it. I talked to your parents before you even arrived here—just to find out what sorts of things you've done before. I understand you like adventures!"

"You got that right!" Johnnie said, as he grinned.

"Well, it looks like you're strapped in and ready to go. Let's see, you've got your gloves, hat, goggles, outriggers and a big smile. I'm going to use these handles that have been fastened onto the back of your seat, and we're going to take the Mitey Mite hand tow up to the first slope of the day. Ready?"

Johnnie gulped.

"Tell you what, Johnnie, let's go to the top and just watch some of the other skiers for awhile."

Together Gary and Johnnie ascended the slope to where the lift ended. At the top, Johnnie saw a boy who looked younger than he waiting his turn to start down the mountain. The boy sat in a monoski much like Johnnie's.

"That's Randy," Gary said. "This is the first time he's skied here."

Johnnie studied Randy's face. "He looks scared," he said. "Who's that other guy with him?"

"That's John—Randy's ski instructor. By the looks of it, John is giving Randy some last-minute instructions on how to lean when he wants to turn. Oh look! They're getting ready to ski!"

John got behind Randy's monoski, grabbed the handles that were attached to the seat and pushed forward.

"Randy doesn't look happy," Johnnie remarked. After a few seconds, Johnnie asked, "Why are they zig-zagging instead of skiing straight down?"

"If they were to ski straight down, they'd be going too fast to steer," Gary explained. "See how Randy is using the outriggers to lean one way then the other? That's what you'll do."

"It looks like John is doing all the work," Johnnie said. "He's practically going sideways!"

Gary laughed. "He's helping Randy go in the right

direction—so they don't run into the trees. Until Randy gets the hang of it, John will be right there with him—just like I will be right there for you."

When Randy reached the bottom, he held his outriggers up in the air in celebration. "Can we watch a couple more skiers go down before I try it?"

"Sure!" Gary said.

One skier toppled over in the monoski. He didn't have an instructor with him. But he was securely strapped in the seat. After a lot of effort, and with the use of the outriggers, the skier managed to get back upright and continued down the slope.

Gary said, "You see, Johnnie, even if you fall, you can get back up. But that's part of everything we'll teach you. And, if that person had continued having trouble getting up, one of us would have gone down to lend a hand."

Finally, Johnnie felt ready. He and Gary headed to the starting spot.

"Whoa!" Johnnie remarked. "When I saw the top of the lift from the bottom, it didn't seem very high. But now that I'm up here looking down…"

"Do you think skiing down this slope is worth the courage it will take to overcome your fears?" Gary asked.

Johnnie thought a moment then said, "Definitely!"

"Then let's do it!"

With that, Gary grabbed the handles on the back of Johnnie's monoski and pushed forward. The air rushed past Johnnie's face as they moved from side to side. Gary would shout to lean right, and Johnnie leaned with all his might. Then Gary would yell out, "Lean left!"

The snow sprayed around him, and the cold, fresh air filled his lungs. It felt as if he were the only person on the mountain. "Yee-haw!" Johnnie yelled as they wound their way to the bottom. "Let's do it again."

For two hours, Johnnie swished down the snowy slope, then he said, "Let's use the chair lift and go higher!"

Gary grinned. "I thought you looked like the adventurous type."

Maneuvering into the chair lift took more effort than hanging onto the hand tow. Each seat connected to a suspended track that slowly moved up and down the mountainside like a conveyer belt. Skiers eased into the seat when the chair dipped down low enough to the ground for them to "catch a ride."

"Let's make sure you are tight in your ski seat," Gary

told Johnnie.

Satisfied that Johnnie was secure, Gary led Johnnie to the chairlifts. Gary walked up to a man who was helping people onto the lift. "This is Charlie. He and I are going to help slide you into the seat. Turn with your back to the chairlift, and as it comes up behind you, we'll slide you in. Grab the bar, and then I'll hop on beside you," he said.

In just a few seconds, Gary smiled and said, "Here comes your lift. Just relax."

The edge of the chair nudged Johnnie's seat. Before he knew it, he and Gary lifted off the ground and rode higher and higher over the mountain slope.

"See those, sharply pointed peaks over there," Gary said as they rode higher up the mountain. "Those are the Bear Tooth Mountains. They sort of look like teeth, don't they?"

Johnnie nodded as he gripped the sidebar of the chairlift.

Within a few minutes, they reached the lift's end. Gary slid out of the seat, onto the snow and then helped Johnnie slide out too. They moved away from the chairlift area.

Johnnie stared at the trail before him. "I should have just ridden the chairlift down," he muttered.

Gary patted him on the back. "Don't worry, Johnnie. This will be a piece of cake. Remember everything I taught you about moving side to side and using the outriggers for balance. I'll be with you every step—er—swish of the way. Ready?"

Johnnie closed his eyes and swallowed hard. With all the adventures he'd been on with his friends at Gun Lake, his hesitation to fly down a mountainside on a monoski surprised him. But determination won out.

"Ready!" Johnnie yelled out.

After the initial rush of adrenaline wore off, Johnnie concentrated on using his body weight to help control where he went. He was tempted to look back to see what Gary was doing, but he kept his focus on the trail ahead. The trees seemed to be racing toward him. Just when he thought he was going to plow into them, he felt himself being pushed in another direction.

"Thank you, Gary!" Johnnie whispered to himself.

Finally, they reached the bottom. Johnnie was out of breath from the sheer excitement of his experience. He looked up in time to see Danny wave at him from the chairlift. All of a sudden, he heard a small yelp and saw Robyn tumble a few feet away from him, landing on her face down in the snow. She rolled over and spit snow out of her mouth.

Johnnie chuckled. "Are you okay?"

Robyn got back up on her skis and dusted herself up. "That was awesome!" she said.

"When do you think I can ski by myself?" Johnnie asked Gary.

He thought for a moment then answered, "Let's see how you do tomorrow. If you're ready, you can solo on the lower slope. Prove yourself there, and we'll talk about the next challenge."

For the rest of the day, Johnnie worked hard and became more skillful. Gary had him practice falling and getting up too. It wasn't nearly as scary as Johnnie thought it would be.

Evening came and Johnnie felt tired but happy. When everyone had gathered back at the lodge, Johnnie exclaimed, "I did it! I really did it! Can we ski again tomorrow?"

Johnnie's father grinned. "Sure! And we can ski all the next day too. But on Monday, we thought we'd go ghost-town hunting over at Virginia City."

"Ghost town!" Johnnie said, as he looked at Danny, Katy and Robyn. "Cool!"

## CHAPTER 5

# A Living Ghost Town

By the time Monday came, Johnnie had skied solo seven times—and fallen eleven times. He rubbed his shoulder. "I think I'm ready for a little break in skiing," he admitted to his father.

"Then let's have something to eat and hunt down some ghosts!" Mr. Jacobson said.

After a hearty breakfast, the families caravanned southwest toward Yellowstone National Park on the Bear Tooth Highway.

"We keep winding our way up," Mrs. Jacobson complained. "How much higher can this mountain go?"

"According to the map, it's about a mile straight up," Mr. Jacobson answered.

As they neared the top, the bag of unopened potato chips Johnnie held in his lap suddenly burst open.

"Whoa!" Johnnie cried. "Maybe those ghosts we heard a about want me to eat some chips!"

Mr. Jacobson laughed. "Well, could be, but I think it has more to do with the altitude. We're about 11,000 feet above sea level, and the air is very thin. That means the air pressure outside the bag is less than the pressure inside the bag. And so, pop goes the potato chips!"

It was Johnnie's turn to laugh.

Elsa suddenly pointed out the window at the sides of the highway. "Look at all that pink rock," she said.

"That's called *Archean gneiss¸* and it's the oldest type of rock in the world," Mr. Jacobson said. "We have some of it in Michigan, and Australia and Siberia have some of it too."

"Okay, I'm impressed," Mrs. Jacobson said. "How did you know all that?"

Mr. Jacobson flashed a sheepish grin. "I read about it in one of the tourist brochures."

"Why is it pink?" Corry asked.

"When the scum off the molten lava, which formed these mountains, cooled, it turned a pinkish color," her father answered.

The Jacobsons stared silently out the windows at the

breathtaking view. Ponderosa pines towered on either side of the road, and incredible rock formations—all frosted with white snow—jutted out at various angles.

"Looks like we're heading out of Yellowstone," Mr. Jacobson announced, as they departed through the park's West Entrance. We're heading into what is called Earthquake Country."

"I remember reading about this area in one of the brochures back at the lodge," Mrs. Jacobson said. "Back in the late summer of 1959, just before midnight, one of the worst earthquakes ever recorded on the North American continent occurred here. Roads suddenly disappeared. A wall of water two stories high stormed over the dam and rushed down the Madison River. Many campers were drowned. The entire side of the mountain crashed down into the canyon, killing even more people. The tumbling rock became crushed, and people say it flowed like water up the other side of the canyon. It dammed up the Madison River and created Quake Lake."

"It doesn't look like anyone lives around here," Johnnie remarked. "Miles and miles of mountains and trees, but no homes."

"No shopping malls either," Elsa grumbled.

Mrs. Jacobson smiled. "It won't be long before we're in Virginia City. I'm sure there'll be some little shops for you to browse in."

\* \* \*

After traveling down through the Madison River Valley and up again through yet another mountain pass, the three families finally reached Virginia City.

They pulled up in front of a large two-story house. "Looks like a museum," Corrie said.

"This is the Bennett House Country Inn," Mr. Jacobson said, as he helped Johnnie out of the van.

Danny, Katy and Robyn hopped out of their van, and ran to meet their friend. "Guess what?" Katy said. "We get to stay here!"

"I don't see any ramps," Johnnie said. "How am I supposed to get up these steps?"

"Well, Johnnie," Mr. Jacobson began. "This is an 1879 Victorian-style house that was converted into an inn. But there is a  guest log cabin that we're going to stay in, so we won't have to climb any stairs."

"A log cabin!" exclaimed Johnnie. "And we'll all fit?"

"It's a big log cabin, and yes, we'll all fit—a little snuggly. But then who's going to stay inside the cabin all day?" Mr. Jacobson said.

"Hey! I thought this was supposed to be a ghost town," Robyn said. "How can *people* live in a ghost town?"

"Let's check in and ask someone," Mrs. Anderson suggested.

While the dads went inside the inn, Johnnie and his friends decided to find the log cabin on their own. The afternoon sky was clear, and the roads and sidewalks were free of snow, which made wheelchair traveling much easier.

"I bet the cabin is behind the house." Katy pointed down a narrow sidewalk that led to the backyard.

As they made their way down the walk, they saw the cabin nestled among some pine trees. Smoke drifted lazily out of the chimney.

"Do you think someone's in there?" Katy asked.

"No." A woman's voice came from behind them. "We just started the fire to warm up the cabin for your arrival."

Johnnie turned and saw a short lady wearing a long

leather coat walking toward him. Her sandy-colored hair showed a few wisps of gray, and she wore it back in a pony tail. Her blue eyes sparkled, and her smile etched creases into her tanned face.

"Welcome to Virginia City," she said. "My name is Annie. I'll show you folks the cabin and try to answer any questions you might have about the town."

She stepped ahead of them and ambled toward the cabin. She unlocked the door.

"Come on in!" she invited.

Johnnie wheeled himself inside. Antique pots and pans and mining tools hung on the walls and from the heavy wooden beams across the high ceiling.. The huge stone fireplace, built into a side wall in the main room, blazed. The sofas, chairs, a round table and, surprisingly, an entertainment center gave the room an odd "modern-antique" appearance.

"There are three large bedrooms, each with its own bathroom," Annie said. "And you'll find a kitchen complete with dishes and pots and pans, if you want to do some of your own cooking. Breakfast is on us, up at the house every morning. If there's anything I can do to help make your stay easier, or if you have any questions about the area, let me know."

Katy looked around then said, "This sure doesn't look like a ghost town to me!"

"Oh, it's a ghost town, all right," Annie said. "When gold was discovered in the mountains, people flocked to Montana. Our gold played a very important role in the Civil War, but I'll get to that later.

"The town we now call Virginia City flourished," she continued. "People built Victorian-style mining camps, which still stand to this day. When the gold became difficult to find, people moved on. But fortunately, the gold didn't run out completely, so the town wasn't totally deserted. Oh yes, there are plenty of ghost stories. And there's more than a few ghosts wandering the streets."

Johnnie saw Danny's eyes gleam in anticipation. Robyn paced around the floor like a nervous cat. "Can we go inside some of these homes?" Robyn asked.

"Sure can!" Annie replied. "Tomorrow morning, about ten o'clock, you can join a tour."

"You mentioned the Civil War," Danny said. "I thought the war was fought between the northern and southern states on the East Coast."

"It's true that most of the famous battles took place

in that area of the country, but most historians will tell you that the Civil War was won based on money and resources rather than on battle strategy," Annie said.

"Believe it or not, Montana was a Confederate state located in Union territory. At the time the Civil War was near its peak, miners were digging up eighteen million dollars worth of gold per week. The Union used that gold to print 'greenbacks,'—their paper money. Then they used the money to build factories and to provide the weapons and materials necessary to win the war. Meanwhile, the South's economy suffered."

"Is it because Montana was a Confederate state that they named this town Virginia City?" Johnnie asked.

"Excellent question!" Annie said. "Actually, the settlers wanted to name the town Varina, after the wife of Jefferson Davis, the President of the Confederate States. But the judge, who approved the establishment of towns, was from Connecticut, a northern state. He said no way to the name Varina, but did say they could call it Virginia. And so that's how we got the name Virginia City."

"Are there still miners who live here?" Katy asked.

Annie grinned. "A few, but I doubt you'll see them in

the wintertime."

"Mom, Dad, the streets are pretty clear," Johnnie said. "Can Danny, Katy, Robyn and I—and Elsa and Corry, if they want to—do some exploring?"

The parents had a quick meeting among themselves, then Mr. Jacobson said, "All right—as long as you stay on the main street and are back by five o'clock."

Corry and Elsa decided to unpack and explore the small shops with their mothers, and the dads opted to settle in front of the fire and check out the television.

Johnnie and his friends headed down the street toward the "ghost end" of town.

"Look!" Johnnie said. "A place to rent snowmobiles! You know, I noticed a forest just outside of town. Do you think our parents will let us do some exploring?"

"Katy, Robyn and I have done snowmobiling in Michigan. They could take one and you and I could take another one," Danny suggested. "Maybe if we took my dad's cell phone, they'd let us go!"

" I don't know why," Johnnie said, "but I have a weird feeling about that forest."

CHAPTER 6

# The Shack in the Forest

"It's Tuesday!" Johnnie yelled. "Time for breakfast and then the tour."

He heard the water running from one of the showers. Everyone seemed to stir and amble out of bed at about the same time.

Johnnie wheeled himself up the sidewalk toward the house. The three dads helped ease the chair backward up the steps and into the elegant foyer of the house.

"Isn't this beautiful?" Mrs. Randall remarked. "I just love the lace curtains and the crystal chandeliers."

"Me too," Mrs. Anderson agreed. "And look at the paintings on the wall. They must be portraits of some of the people who used to live here."

Johnnie's nose twitched. "I smell bacon!" he said. "Can we eat and *then* admire the house?"

Everyone laughed. Mrs. Randall said, "I have to admit, that food does smell inviting. Let's head to the dining room."

More curtains, chandeliers, paintings and delicate wallpaper adorned the room. But what caught Johnnie's attention was the dining room table, set with real china and silverware, just waiting for them to sit down and eat.

"Breakfast will be served family style," Annie said. "We'll bring in the food, put it on the table, and let everyone help themselves."

Pancakes, bacon, eggs, toast and jelly and juices were offered. Johnnie sampled everything.

When everyone's stomachs registered full, they thanked their hostess and headed for the door. Annie smiled and said, "The wagon for the tour will be here in just five minutes. Enjoy your day!"

"About how long does the tour last?" Danny asked.

"Oh, about two hours," Annie replied. "If you want to stop at the local grocery store before coming back, just tell the driver. You can pick up lunch or even dinner items there."

\* \* \*

The horse-drawn wagon lumbered up the street. The

freezing morning air stung Johnnie's face, yet the sun warmed him so he unzipped his jacket. As the wagon creaked through the town streets, the driver, whose name was Jack, pointed out areas of interest.

"Notice the wooden sidewalks that run through the town," Jack noted.  "And if you recognize any of these buildings but can't remember why they look so familiar, it may be because you saw them in a Western movie."

"Cool!" Johnnie said.

"Now, over to your right, you'll see the 1876 court-house. As you can tell, there are a number of different styles of buildings and homes here. And, the people you see walking around are real—not ghosts!" Jack chuckled as he turned the corner.

When they came to a block of homes, Jack explained, "These homes are on the Creighton Block. The building on the left-hand side of the row was built during the Civil War by a man named J. M. Lewis. We really don't know anything about him other than he built that house out of log-like posts and wood planks, just like the other ones."

Jack pulled up next to the house. "Let's take a little stop here and examine one of those wood planks," he said.

The group crowded around the area of the house where Jack stood, pointing. "See that picture? It was drawn in pencil by a Union soldier during the Civil War."

Johnnie stared at the antique drawing of what looked like an eagle with a banner in its mouth. "What do those words on the banner mean?" he asked.

"That's a Latin phrase—*e pluribus unum*—which means 'one out of many.' It's our nation's motto, meaning one country out of many states. If you look on a one-dollar bill, you will see an eagle with a banner that has those words on it," Jack said.

The group filed back into the wagon. Before they left the Lewis house, Jack said, "That house was sold to a George Gohn in 1870. He was a butcher by trade, and he was also a Vigilante."

"Vigilante!" Danny's mouth dropped open. "Did Vigilantes go around hanging people?"

"They sure did," Jack replied. "But there was a reason why the Vigilantes became so powerful. Back in the gold rush days, this city buzzed with miners. And it also buzzed with crooks—people who would steal or even kill to get someone else's gold. The sheriff wouldn't do a thing about it. Most people believe the sheriff was the head of these thieves. We call them 'outlaws.'

"Anyway," Jack continued, "citizens became sick and tired of all the crime, and so they decided to take the law into their own hands. And as the Civil War progressed, Virginia City became the center of activity for the Vigilantes. What started out as trying to maintain law and order got out of control. It was said that Vigilantes would accuse, convict and execute people for just being annoying drunks!

"Eventually, the Vigilantes became worried that they might be arrested for murder, so they ran and covered their tracks the best they could. There are a lot of stories and rumors, but no one seems to know for sure all that really went on."

Johnnie's mind whirled: Ghost towns. Vigilantes. Union and Confederate soldiers. Gold. "Oh yeah," he muttered to himself, "we have *got* to do some exploring."

\* \* \*

When the tour ended and everyone headed back to the cabin, Danny, Katy, Robyn and Johnnie huddled in a corner next to the fireplace. "I heard my mom say that the women were going shopping," Johnnie whispered. "I'm sure my sisters will want to go with them."

"And my dad said he wanted to walk around the town some more," Robyn said.

"Mine too!" Katy quipped.

Johnnie grinned. "Let's ask them about the snowmobiles. I mean, shopping and walking around the town are b-o-r-i-n-g!"

"All right," Mr. Jacobson called out. "What are you kids up to over there?"

So Johnnie and the rest of the kids told their parents their plan. After about fifteen minutes of bargaining, consent was finally given.

"Take my cell phone," Mr. Randall instructed. "If anything happens, call Mr. Jacobson's cell phone."

"And stay on well-marked trails," Mrs. Randall reminded them.

Mrs. Anderson stood in the kitchen holding a loaf of bread they had purchased at the grocery store. "First, let's have some quick sandwiches. Then the dads can drop you off at the snowmobile rental place, while we ladies do some serious shopping!"

\* \* \*

Mr. Randall's watch read five minutes after one o'clock. "Okay, kids," he said. "We'll be back here at 3:30 to pick you up. Danny, do you have your watch?"

Danny pushed up the left sleeve of his jacket and showed his dad his watch.

"What time does your watch read?" his dad asked.

"It's one-o-five…er, make that one-o-six," Danny answered.

"Good!" Mr. Randall said. "Our watches are in synch, so there should be no reason that you shouldn't be back here on time. Right?"

"Right!"

The fathers split the rental costs of the two-seater snowmobiles and watched as the kids mounted them.

"Stick to the main streets and snowmobile trails," the rental man said.

Danny and Katy fired up the motors. Johnnie and Robyn, each seated on the backs of the snowmobiles, secured their sunglasses and prepared for "take off."

The kids smiled and waved as they headed down the side of the street.

Johnnie breathed a huge sigh of relief. "On our own

at last!" he yelled over the noise of the motors.

The road curved gently and followed the forest. They learned that they weren't too far from Beaverhead National Park—in fact they were on the very outskirts of the heavily treed forest.

Danny and Katy came to a stop and turned off the motors. "The guy at the snowmobile place said people usually backpack in and out of the forest," Danny said.

"There must be *some* trails in here," Robyn said. "It looks pretty dense with trees, but I think we could wind our way around."

"Hey Danny!" Johnnie said. "How about letting me drive for awhile? I can balance myself with my knees on the runners, and the controls look like the ones I use on my jetski."

"Sure!" Danny said, as he traded places with Johnnie. The snowmobiles' engines roared into action, and Johnnie and Katy skillfully steered them into the forest.

"Ouch!" Robyn yelled, as the snowmobile bounced over a fallen tree branch.

"Sorry!" Katy called back over her shoulder.

After zig-zagging around trees, rocks and fallen branches for a half hour, Johnnie and Katy turned off the motors.

"We've been steadily climbing," Danny said. "The mountain air makes it a little difficult to breath! Let's stop and rest."

"We're not lost, are we?" Robyn asked. She looked up. "All I can see are treetops."

"We haven't crossed any of our own snowmobile tracks," Danny said. "So all we have to do backtrack starting around 2:20, and we'll end up where we started!"

"Hey!" Johnnie cried. He pointed toward an opening of trees just off to the left of where they were. "It looks like a clearing of some sort. Let's find out what's there."

The two snowmobiles glided toward the clearing. Just before they reached it, Katy stopped and pointed up toward a tree. They cut the engines. "Look!" she said. "There's a sign up there: BEWARE!"

"Looks pretty old to me," Johnnie commented.

Suddenly, Robyn let out a yelp. "Look over in that other tree! What is that thing hanging there?"

The kids stared hard at the tree. "It looks like a bear's skull!" Danny said. "And look! There's a shack!"

They all looked at each other. A grin flashed across

Johnnie's face. "Well, what are we waiting for? Let's go!"

CHAPTER 7

# Footprints!

The snowmobiles sprang into action as Johnnie and Katy led the way into the clearing. There, partly hidden by some pine trees, sat the old wooden shack.

"It looks sort of like some of those old houses we saw in the city—only more run down," Robyn said. "Do you think any of those Vigilante people are hiding there?"

"Let's go look inside," Johnnie said.

"I wish these snowmobiles didn't make so much noise," Robyn said. "If anybody is in there, he is going to know we're coming."

"With all the noise we've made so far, winding our way up here, if there's somebody living there, he already knows we're on our way," Danny pointed out.

Katy took a deep breath and started her snowmobile. Johnnie did likewise. They slowly headed toward the shack. The wood looked old, like it had never been painted. The glass windows were unbroken and reflected the forest scene behind them.

"No porch or steps!" Johnnie commented.

"There are some prints in the snow!" exclaimed Katy. She pulled up parallel to the shack so Robyn could see.

"Just small animal tracks," Robyn noted. "Oh! And look over there. Deer tracks."

The telltale two-hoofed tracks indicated that several deer had explored the area rather recently.

"Drive up to the door, Johnnie," said Danny. "Let's see if it's open."

Johnnie maneuvered the snowmobile within a few inches of the front door. Danny reached out and turned the knob. It wasn't locked. Carefully, he pulled the door open.

A musty odor greeted his nose, mixed with another smell he couldn't identify. "Robyn, could you go and look inside?" Johnnie asked.

Reluctantly, Robyn slid off the back of the snowmobile and tiptoed toward the house, her boots making a light crunching noise in the snow. She reached the front door and peered inside.

"There aren't anymore windows in here, so it's kind of dim," she called back over her shoulder. She stepped inside and then came back out. "It looks like someone may be living here!"

"Well, what's in there?" Johnnie asked.

"Just a table and chair and a bed. But there are pans and some sort of dishes too. Plus a big fireplace with a pot sitting on the logs."

Robyn ventured farther into the shack. In a few moments she hurriedly came out again. "There is definitely someone living here," she said. "I saw blankets and some food scraps. And, there's a backdoor!"

"Backdoor!" Johnnie cried, as he put the snowmobile in gear and headed around the side of the cabin.

Katy followed on her snowmobile while Robyn ran beside her.

"Whoa! Look at these footprints!" Johnnie cried.

"Shh!" Robyn cautioned. "Someone could be lurking around here. These prints are huge! And what a weird shape. What do you..."

"Look over there!" Johnnie whispered, interrupting Robyn.

They all looked into the woods.

"What?" Danny said. "I don't see anything."

"I saw something big and furry moving over in that direction," Johnnie said.

"B-big and furry?" Katy stammered. "Like a grizzly b-bear?"

Johnnie thought for a moment. "It *could* have been a bear, but I thought bears hibernate during the winter."

"Look at these tracks," Danny said. "It looks like whatever it is walks on two feet."

"Maybe it's the abdominal snowman," Katy said, her eye's widening.

Danny laughed. "That's *abominable* snowman! And I don't believe they even exist."

"Well, believe it or not, I just saw it again going down that hill," said Johnnie.

Danny looked at the pathway through the trees. Then he looked at his watch. "It's two o'clock. We'll have to start heading back soon."

"Okay, okay!" Johnnie said. "We'll head back soon. But for now, let's try to catch up with that—thing!"

Danny hesitated. "Come on!" Johnnie practically shouted. "We wanted an adventure, and here it is just a few feet away!"

"Okay!" Danny agreed. "Let's go!"

## CHAPTER 8

# The Chase

Johnnie and Katy kept the snowmobiles in the lowest gear and slowly followed the footprints in the snow. Danny and Robyn, astride the back of the vehicles, kept a sharp lookout for signs of "the creature"—the nickname they gave whatever it was they were following.

Suddenly Johnnie held up his hand and indicated for Katy to stop. "Over there!" he said, and pointed to a grove of trees just ahead of them.

Suddenly, Johnnie caught a glimpse of something furry moving swiftly through the woods.

"It looks like he's headed down a hill," Johnnie said. "Come on! Hurry! He's getting away!"

He cranked up the snowmobile's engine and took off with a jolt. The crisp, thin air made Johnnie breathless as they wove their way in and out of pine trees. Johnnie could feel Danny cling to his jacket.

Bare, low branches made the obstacle course even more treacherous. Johnnie's sunglasses protected his eyes, and his clothes protected his skin from the small branches and pinecones that flew up as the snowmobile raced on.

Johnnie pressed his vehicle to the limit, and the two boys bounced along the snow-covered bumpy forest floor. All of a sudden, they hit a half-buried tree stump. The snowmobile leapt into the air. Johnnie felt his body slide to the right, while the snowmobile careened to the left.

The next thing Johnnie knew, he was rolling down a small slope. A thin pine tree stopped his downward journey with a jolt.

He looked around and saw Danny sprawled face down on the hill, just a few feet away. The snowmobile had landed farther down the slope on its side. The motor automatically had shut down when Johnnie had released his grip on the throttle.

"Danny!" Johnnie yelled. He used his arms to crawl, army style, through the snow toward his friend.

Just then, he heard the motor of Katy's snowmobile,

as it crested the hill. Katy and Robyn carefully made their way down the hill toward the place where Danny lay. They reached Danny just ahead of Johnnie. Katy cut the motor and leapt off the snowmobile. She rushed over to her brother. Robyn, likewise, jumped off the backseat and ran over to Johnnie.

"Johnnie!" she cried. "Are you all right?"

"Yeah, I'm fine," he said. "What about Danny?"

By the time Johnnie and Robyn reached Danny, he had rolled over onto his back, looking a little dazed.

"Whoa!" Danny said. "What did we hit back there?"

He sat up slowly and blinked. "Where's the snowmobile?"

"Down the hill a few yards," Katy said, wiping tears from her eyes. "Do you think you broke anything? I thought you were—well, you know."

"What? You thought I was dead?" Danny said. He patted Katy on the back. "Nah! I can't die before we solve this mystery." He smiled and slowly stood. Then he danced around a little in the snow.

"See?" he said. "I'm fine. I just hope the snowmobile is fine."

"I'll go down the hill with you to check," Robyn

offered. "Johnnie, you and Katy wait here. Hopefully, we'll ride the snowmobile back up to get you."

Danny and Robyn eased their way to the fallen snowmobile. With a strong tug, they pulled it back up onto its runners. Danny checked it over for damage.

He yelled up to where Johnnie was waiting. "It looks fine. Let's see if it still runs!"

He pushed the starter button and the engine fired right up. Danny smiled, and Robyn hopped onto the back for the ride back up the hill.

Robyn rejoined Katy, while Johnnie lifted himself onto the back of the other vehicle.

"I feel a little shaky," Johnnie said. "You drive for awhile."

Danny looked at his watch. "Oh no! It's 2:30! We should head back."

"Let's just go down to the bottom of the hill," Johnnie pleaded. "The footprints lead down there. If we can't see anything, then we can head back."

Danny sighed. "Well, I guess we've come *this* far." He put the snowmobile in gear and glided down the hill and into another patch of trees. The footprints were wide apart. "He's running!" Danny shouted.

"Over there!" Robyn yelled, pointing to an area that looked like a clearing.

Sure enough, the furry creature was running in a zig-zag fashion. Then all of a sudden, it dropped out of sight.

Johnnie gasped. "Where did he go? "Let's follow him—but slowly."

Danny led the way, keeping the snowmobile next to the set of tracks. As they came close to the clearing, a sudden gust of cold wind nearly took away Johnnie's breath.

"Slow down!" Johnnie yelled. "I think we're coming to the edge of a cliff."

Both Danny and Katy slowed to a crawl. They inched their way toward the clearing. Suddenly, straight ahead of them were other mountain peaks and graying sky. The trail they had been following abruptly ended at the cliff's edge.

They stopped, and Robyn eased herself off the seat. She carefully walked toward the edge and peered over it.

"Oh!" she yelped, and jumped back. "It's almost straight down. Definitely not a good snowmobile trail."

Johnnie slipped off the back of his seat and slid on his

stomach toward the edge. He too peered over the edge.

"Danny! Come quick! I think we've found our creature!"

CHAPTER 9

# The Ravine

Johnnie took off his sunglasses so he could see better. Danny, Robyn and Katy crouched beside him and looked down into a shallow ravine, where the creature lay, its back to them.

"Do you think it's dead?" Katy whispered.

"I don't know," Johnnie whispered back.

"Look!" Robyn's voice sounded shaky. "I thought I saw its head move."

Johnnie inched further toward the edge. Danny hung onto Johnnie's jacket—just in case.

"I see an arm!" Robyn yelled.

Johnnie sensed Danny tighten his grip on his jacket, as the creature turned over onto its back.

"Wait a minute!" Danny said, loosening his grip. "That's not a creature. It—I mean *he*—is a man!"

"Are you sure?" Katy asked, backing away from the cliff's edge.

Danny responded, "Yes, and he looks hurt."

He cupped his hands around his mouth and yelled down to the man, "Hey! Are you all right?"

The man waved his arms and pointed to his leg.

"I think his leg must be hurt," Johnnie said. "Danny, you're going to have to go down there and find out how badly he's injured."

"I have a better idea," Danny said, as he reached into his pocket. "I'll call our dads, and tell them what's happening. Then they can call the ski patrol or rescue squad, and *they* can rescue that man."

Katy breathed a sigh of relief. "For a minute there, I thought you were actually going to try to go down into that ravine."

Johnnie saw Danny check his pockets and look around. "Uh-oh," Johnnie said. "Don't tell me you lost the cell phone."

Danny's face was pale. "Oh no!" he moaned. "It must have fallen out of my pocket when we crashed landed. Katy, you and I had better go back and look for it. Johnnie, can you and Robyn stay here and keep an eye on that guy?"

Johnnie looked up into the wintry sky. The wind swirled snow into his face. "I don't like the looks of those gray clouds moving in," he said. "You and Katy had better hurry."

"Let's just take one snowmobile," Danny suggested. "We'll leave the other one here, in case you need it."

Johnnie watched as Danny and Katy drove back through the grove of trees and up the slope.

Robyn tugged at Johnnie's sleeve. "Look! He's motioning for us to come down."

"No way!" Johnnie said. "If we go down, how do we know we'll be able to get back up?"

"It really doesn't look *that* steep," Robyn argued. "If I go down sideways, I bet I could reach him safely. It's quite a ways down—if nothing else, I could slide on my bottom!"

"You're not going down there without me!" Johnnie stated emphatically. "If you can slide, then so can I."

"Yes, but then how are you going to get back up?" Robyn looked Johnnie in the eyes. "We won't be able to slide *up* the hill."

Johnnie thought for a moment. "Good point," he

said finally.

Johnnie remembered what Gary had said to him when he faced skiing down the mountain for the first time. So, he decided to say the same thing to Robyn. "Do you think going down to the man is worth the courage it will take to overcome your fears?"

Robyn looked surprised, and then said, "Yes!"

"Then do it!" Johnnie smiled.

Robyn lowered herself over the slightly protruding ledge of the cliff. She slid partway down the slope but was able to grab onto a nearby pine.

The wind began howling as its intensity increased. Johnnie knew a storm was on the way. He saw Robyn look up at him before she began her descent again. He waved at her and yelled, "Keep going. You're doing fine!"

Robyn waved back and nodded that she understood. Johnnie noted that she kept her feet parallel to the slope, moving sideways like a hermit crab farther and farther down. Trees dotted the route she took to the ravine. Robyn connected with several of them to help slow her downward progress.

Just as she reached the bottom, it started to snow. Johnnie saw Robyn kneel next to the man. He moved slowly and pointed at his leg. Robyn yelled up at Johnnie, and through the eerie sound of the wind he heard her say, "He needs help!"

Behind him, Johnnie heard the noise of Danny's snowmobile engine as it glided closer to him. He turned and saw Danny and Katy maneuvering through the trees.

Danny's face was flushed and he was out of breath. Katy, too, looked exhausted.

"We looked everywhere," Danny said as he panted for air. "No use. The cell phone is gone."

"Where's Robyn?" Katy asked. Her eyes widened. "What happened?" she yelled. "Did she fall over the cliff?"

"No, she's all right," Johnnie reassured her. "She decided she had to go down and check out our furry friend."

"How do we know he's a friend?" demanded Danny. "She should never have gone down there by herself. I'd better get down there."

Without another word, Danny slowly eased himself over the edge of the cliff and inched his way down the slope, much like Robyn had.

Swirls of snow, both from the already snow-covered mountains and from the clouds above, spun around Johnnie and Katy, as they strained to see what was going on below them. Danny joined Robyn in the ravine. Robyn held the man's head in her lap, and Danny checked the man's leg. In a few moments, Danny began heading back up the slope.

Johnnie watched as Danny grabbed onto trees and crawled on all fours upward. A couple of times he slipped back a few feet, but he regained his footing and finally trudged back to where his sister and Johnnie waited.

Johnnie lay on his stomach and extended an arm to Danny as he drew near the top. Katy hung onto Johnnie's legs, as Johnnie pulled Danny up the remaining few feet.

"Well?" Katy demanded. "What is going on down there?"

"Danny rolled over onto his back, gasping for air. "Give me a second," he wheezed. A few moments later, he sat up and panted out the words, "Gotta get them out of there. Man is hurt. Storm's coming."

"How are we going to get them out of that ravine?"

Katy asked. She paced nervously in the snow, oblivious to how close she was to the cliff's edge.

"We don't have any telephone. We can't just carry the man up. The snowmobiles won't make it down there safely. And a storm is brewing," she said. "What are we going to do?"

"Think," Johnnie muttered to himself. "Think! We've got to think of something fast."

## CHAPTER 10

# Rescue from the Ravine

Just then Johnnie heard a deep rumble coming from the mountains. "Thunder!?" he asked in surprise. But the sound of the thunder gave him an idea.

"Danny, can you and Katy find your way back to the shack?"

"Sure!" Danny said. "But what good will that do us. I doubt if he has a telephone."

"Not a telephone," Johnnie said. "But rope. If he's got pots and pans and bedding, then I'll bet he has rope."

"I'm not sure the four of us could pull him up that slope," Katy said. "Four adults, maybe—but I'm not exactly buff, if you know what I mean."

"Do you think a snowmobile might be powerful enough?" asked Johnnie.

Danny smiled. "Yes!" he shouted. "Come on, Katy, let's find some sturdy rope."

Katy hopped back onto the snowmobile, and in an instant she and Danny were weaving their way back toward the shack.

Johnnie looked down at Robyn and the man. Then he cupped his hands around his mouth. "We're getting help," he yelled above the sound of the wind.

Robyn looked up and waved, but Johnnie wasn't sure whether she heard him. The ground felt cold and moist under him, so Johnnie decided to make his way back over to the other snowmobile. Once there, he pulled himself up onto the seat.

The snow began falling faster, blowing in whatever direction the wind took it. Johnnie pulled his jacket tighter around him. The darkening sky looked angry, and the thunder boomed closer.

Feeling helpless and alone, Johnnie prayed for their safety—especially for Robyn and the man, who were at the bottom of the ravine.

"And God," Johnnie added after a moment of silence, "please keep the noise down on that thunder. It's scary enough without all the ka-booms!"

As if in answer, a low rumble of thunder faded into the mountains. Then just a few moments later, a louder rumble came. Johnnie turned and saw Danny and Katy heading swiftly toward him, a huge coil of rope draped over Katy. Johnnie had to chuckle.

"What's so funny?" Katy asked.

"You look like one of those snakes in India, coiling your way out of a rope basket," Johnnie answered.

Katy rolled her eyes. "Leave it to you to come up with some warped humor. Now get me out of here!"

Danny laughed. "Sit still, Katy. I'll get it off of you."

Johnnie looked at the rope. "Do you think it will be long enough to go down the entire slope?"

"I doubt it," Danny said. "But look what else we found." Katy jumped off the snowmobile. Folded under her was a large piece of tarp.

Johnnie couldn't resist one more remark. "Wow, you're a regular cargo bay, Katy!"

Even Katy had to laugh at that. Then she unfolded the tarp and said, "I think this is big enough for us to put under the man. We also found some bungee cords, to fasten it around him."

"When I went down into the ravine," Danny said,

"there were places toward the bottom that weren't too steep. Let's throw the rope down and see how far it goes. Then we'll know how far we have to pull the man up."

Danny tied one end of the rope securely around the hitch on the back of the snowmobile. Then he threw the rope down over the cliff's edge. It reached almost halfway down.

"That's not very far," Katy said. "I can't imagine us pushing and pulling a grown adult halfway up the slope."

"Here's something else we found that might be useful," Danny said. Out of his pocket he pulled a strap that looked like a dog's leash. On the end of it was a clip designed to fasten onto the collar's ring.

"I get it," Johnnie said. We could fasten the clip through one of the eyelets in the tarp."

"Yes, and then we can tie the rope through the loop at the other end of the dog leash," Danny added.

"But still, how are we going to get that man halfway up the slope?" Katy asked.

"By using the trees," Danny said. "If we get in a position above him, and brace our feet against one of the trees, we'll have enough leverage to pull him up. Then we'll park him in front of the tree so he doesn't slide down, and go up to another tree."

"Then when you're about halfway up, you can bring the rope all the way to the top, and we can hook it up to one of the snowmobiles and pull him the rest of the way," Johnnie said.

"Yes," Danny agreed. "But we won't be able to just rely on the snowmobile. One person will drive the snowmobile and the rest will help pull."

"It's a good plan!" Johnnie said.

"Okay then, if we're ready, let's put it into action," Danny said. "Katy, you're with me."

"And I'll wait up here ready to hook the rope onto the snowmobile," Johnnie said.

Danny led the way as he and Katy half slid down the slope—tarp, bungee cords, rope and leash in hand. The falling snow came down in tiny pellets, which stung Johnnie's face and made it difficult for him to track what was happening.

He saw Danny and Katy reach the man and Robyn. Then everyone scurried around. Katy unfolded the tarp and Robyn and Danny helped the man scoot into the center of it. They folded the sides over and secured it with the bungee cords. Johnnie saw Danny take out the leash and work to secure it to the tarp. So far, so good.

Katy stayed with the man as Robyn and Danny climbed toward the first tree. Katy helped push, while Robyn and Danny, their feet against the trunk of the tree, pulled.

Johnnie, who was sitting astride the snowmobile, felt excited. "Yes!" he yelled. "It's working.

After much effort, the man and his blue tarp "sled" made it to the first tree. Again, Katy stayed with the man while Robyn and Danny carried the rope to the next tree.

Johnnie could see Katy's feet slipping in the snow as she tried to help push. Danny and Robyn pulled hard and slowly the tarp sled moved upward. Johnnie figured they were about a fourth of the way up.

"Just two or three more pulls, and we'll have him," Johnnie said to himself.

Johnnie saw the man holding onto the tarp—probably to help keep himself from sliding out the other end. He motioned to the leash and rope. Johnnie watched as Danny unleashed the tarp and reattached it to an eyelet near one of the bungee cords.

This time, when Danny and Robyn pulled, instead of the man being pulled head-first up the hill, he came up sideways.

Johnnie nodded in approval. "Clever! That will make it less likely that he'll slip out of the bottom of the tarp."

The plan worked. When they reached the third tree, Johnnie's three friends had to rest awhile. A low rumble of thunder seemed to encourage them to once again trudge upward toward what would hopefully be the last tree.

When Johnnie saw they were more than halfway up the slope, he cupped his hands around his mouth and yelled, "I think you can bring the rope up now."

Danny looked up and nodded. After making sure the man was safely tucked next to the tree, Danny and Robyn slowly made their way up the slope. Katy stayed behind.

Through frigid wind and swirling snow, Danny and Robyn clamored over the cliff's edge, with plenty of rope to spare.

"Katy's going to make sure the rope stays secure," Danny panted. "Johnnie, do you want to drive the snow-mobile or help pull up the rope?"

"Hey! I don't know that much about snowmobiles, but after pushing a wheelchair around most of my life, I guess you'd say I'm pretty strong. I'll pull."

"I was hoping you'd say that," Danny said.

Johnnie slid off the snowmobile and moved over to the edge of the cliff. Danny secured the rope to the hitch on the snowmobile. He looked back at Johnnie and Robyn. Johnnie was closest to the cliff, and Robyn held onto the rope a little farther back.

"I'm going to start slowly," Danny told them. "If something goes wrong, yell, and I'll stop. Ready?"

Johnnie and Robyn nodded. Danny started the engine and eased the snowmobile forward. He felt the tug as the rope tightened and picked up the weight of the man.

Johnnie took off his gloves so he could get a better grip on the rope. As Danny inched away from the cliff, Johnnie could see the tarp sled move up. Katy crawled beside the man, watching the leash to make sure it didn't unhook or that the rope didn't become loosened.

Inch by inch, the sled moved upward. Johnnie's hands were beginning to feel numb. The snow stung his face and his eyes. He didn't dare look behind him to see how Robyn was doing. His focus was on the man being pulled up.

After what seemed like hours, the tarp was within grasp. Johnnie yelled for Katy to climb up over the edge of the cliff and help him pull the man up and over the ledge.

Suddenly the snowmobile engine stopped. Johnnie heard Robyn yell out, "Danny's tying the rope around a tree, then I think he'll come and help us. Hang on!"

Sure enough, within moments, both Danny and Robyn were at Johnnie and Katy's side. Together they lifted the sled over the edge and pulled it toward safety.

The man's eyes were blinking as the snow pelted him in the face.

Katy reached over and pulled his fur cap down over his face. "Don't worry, mister," she said. "We'll get you home."

"We don't need this much rope," Danny said. "Let's loop the rope around the handlebars of the snowmobile and bring the sled closer in. Johnnie, you'll have to hang onto the rest of this rope."

"Maybe we should hook his sled up so that we're not pulling him sideways," Johnnie suggested, as he stuffed his hands back into his gloves. "He should be in a straight line behind the snowmobile. I think that would be safer."

"Good idea," Danny agreed. "Katy, you and Robyn ride next to him to make sure he's okay."

"Okay," Robyn said. "While I don't want to take any unnecessary chances, the quicker we get back to the shack the better. It's getting so dark that it's hard to see."

It didn't take long for the kids to shorten the length of the rope and rehook the leash to an eyelet in the tarp close to the man's head. Danny took off slowly to make sure everything was okay. Katy and Robyn rode beside the man with Katy keeping an eye on the trail while Robyn watched the man.

The persistent wind at their backs seemed to push them along toward their destination. And all the way there, Johnnie wondered what their parents were thinking.

CHAPTER 11

# The Storm

The kids wound their way around the trees. Danny did his best to avoid protruding rocks and tree stumps, but the blizzard-like conditions made navigation difficult. The tracks they had made earlier had been swirled away, like someone had taken a huge paintbrush and covered over them.

Tall ponderosa pines swayed in the wind. Every once in a while, Johnnie could hear the overhead branches cracking as the wind broke them. The wind, which at first was at their backs, now whirled around them, pushing them off course and then back on course again.

Johnnie felt the biting cold through his ski jacket. His hands were still numb from the cold.

"How much farther?" Johnnie yelled over the wind.

Danny, who was hunched down over the handlebars, sat up and yelled, "It's just a little farther, over that ridge."

Johnnie felt encouraged. He looked back at the girls. The two were hunched over, trying to stay as low as possible. The man's face was covered by his fur hat, and he looked half-buried in the snow as it flew all around him.

Finally, Johnnie could see the dark outline of the shack. When they reached the front door, Danny and Katy cut the snowmobiles' engines and jumped off. Robyn and Johnnie busily unhooked the tarp sled, though their fingers were stiff.

Danny, Katy and Robyn grabbed a hold of the tarp's edge and pulled the man toward the door, which Johnnie held open. They slid the tarp inside the shack. Danny went back and held the door open so Johnnie could scoot inside.

The two small windows didn't allow much light to filter in. Danny shut the door against the wind and used the wooden bar to secure it.

"I remember some kindling wood in a box by the fireplace," Robyn said.

"And when Katy and I came back for the rope, we

noticed some matches on the mantle," Danny said.

"Where's a flashlight when you need one?" Johnnie asked.

A muffled sound came from the man. "He's trying to say something!" Katy cried. She took the hat off the man's face.

"You'll find a flashlight under the bed," the man said.

Katy scrambled over to the bed, bumping her knee on the table in the process. She knelt and searched for the flashlight with her arm. Sure enough, toward the head of the bed, she found it and quickly clicked it on.

"That's better!" Danny exclaimed. With some light to work with, the kids lost no time in starting the kindling on fire. They added larger pieces of wood, and before long, a warm, friendly fire blazed before them.

Meanwhile, Robyn and Katy freed the man from the bungee-held tarp, and moved him closer to the fire. They took a pillow from his bed and tucked it under his head. With every move, the man moaned in pain.

In the glow of the fire, Johnnie observed that the man's face looked weathered. His eyes were dark, and his long graying hair was tied back with a leather strap. A few wisps stuck out here and there, some of them catching in his bushy beard. He reminded Johnnie of one of the pictures he had seen of the mountain men who lived in the 1870s.

Johnnie suddenly noticed the snow-crusted fur coat the man still wore. "I think we'd better take off his coat. It's all wet from the snow. Are there any blankets on his bed?"

Robyn pulled off a couple of blankets from the bed while Johnnie and Danny worked gingerly to remove the man's coat.

The wind pounded fiercely at the door and windows. One gust blew into the chimney causing the fire to flicker wildly. The shack groaned and creaked as if it were going to fly apart.

"We're going to have to make sure that fire doesn't go out," Johnnie said. "And I don't know if there is enough wood inside to make it through the night. What time is it anyway, Danny?"

Danny held his watch toward the glowing fire. "It's after six!"

Katy gasped. "I had no idea it was that late."

"We've been working at this rescue for nearly four hours!" Robyn said as she collapsed against the bed. "I wonder how long the storm will last."

"I wonder how frantic our parents are," Johnnie said.

The man groaned and tried to move over onto his side.

"Here, let me help you," Katy offered. She took off some more blankets from the bed and rolled them up like a log. Then she stuffed these behind the man to give him some support.

"My mom did that for me once, when I had hurt myself. It felt good," Katy explained.

Johnnie sniffed the air. "What's that smell?" he asked. "It smells like chicken noodle soup—or am I just hallucinating?"

The man grunted. "It is chicken noodle soup," he said. It's in the kettle that's sitting on top of those logs you set on fire. Let the fire die down a bit, and then you can take the ladle off the mantel and spoon some into some bowls. I only have two, so we'll have to share, but it will warm us up a bit."

"By the way," Johnnie said. "When we were following you, what were those weird big tracks we saw in the snow?"

The man laughed a little. "Those were snowshoe

tracks. They equalize your weight so you can practically walk on top of the snow."

"They must have fallen off when you fell," Katy said.

"Yep! They sure did."

"Why were you running away?" Danny asked.

"Well, why were you chasing me?" the man answered.

"We thought you were a furry creature," Katy admitted. "We were on an adventure and, well, you looked pretty interesting."

"We're sorry if we scared you," Danny said.

"Well, you sure did give me a scare," the man admitted. "But I'm really glad you were there to help me after I fell off that cliff. I just wasn't looking where I was going—that's for sure."

Johnnie scooted closer to the man and said, "By the way, my name is Johnnie Jacobson, and these are my friends Danny and Katy Randall and Robyn Anderson."

"Well, my name is Chaz—Chaz King."

"Chaz! Wow, that's a cool name. How'd you ever get that name?" Johnnie asked.

"Well, my real name is Charles, but later on I

changed it to Chaz because *I* thought it sounded cool."

He frowned at Johnnie and asked, "Son, are you all right? Did you get hurt while you were rescuing me?"

Johnnie looked alarmed. "No, I'm fine! At least I *think* I'm fine. Do I look hurt?"

He quickly checked himself over, thinking perhaps he was bleeding somewhere.

"Well, you *look* fine, except I noticed you're not walking," Chaz explained. "Did you hurt your legs?"

Johnnie sighed with relief and smiled. "No, I'm fine—really! I have cerebral palsy and can't walk. Usually I have a wheelchair, but the snowmobile took its place."

"Cerebral palsy!" Chaz exclaimed. "I had a sister who was born with cerebral palsy, but she couldn't talk or hardly move her arms. I remember how my parents had to tie her into a wheelchair and feed her. Eventually, they had to put her in a special home because they couldn't take care of her."

"Well, cerebral palsy affects people differently. It just depends on what part of the brain is affected," Johnnie said. "Fortunately for me, only my legs don't work."

"Sure hope you don't mind my asking about your legs and all," Chaz said.

"Actually, I'm glad you did. What really gets to me, sometimes, are the people who stare at me and talk behind my back. I know they're wondering what happened to me, and I appreciate it when someone has guts enough to ask," Johnnie replied.

"And now," Johnnie continued, "since I've told you a little bit about me, why don't you tell us a little bit about yourself."

"Tell you what," Chaz said, "if you get me a bowl of that soup, I'll tell you my story."

Just then they heard a loud cracking noise from outside, followed by a resounding thud. "I hope that was a tree limb falling and not the beginning of a real-life ghost story," Katy said, as they all jumped.

CHAPTER 12

# Chaz King

Danny ladled some of the steaming soup into a bowl, while Johnnie and Katy pulled the tarp toward the bed. Then Robyn helped Chaz sit up so he could lean against the bed's frame.

Danny found another bowl and ladled some more of the soup for the kids to share. Johnnie hadn't realized how hungry he was until he tasted some of the rich broth and sucked down a couple noodles.

"Mm," Johnnie said. "This is good stuff!"

Everyone agreed.

The wind had died down a bit and Chaz said, "I have a plastic bag somewhere over by the pots and pans. Maybe you should venture out and fill the bag with some snow. Then you can pack the bag around my leg. I think it's broken."

Robyn found the plastic bag, and she and Danny slowly opened the wooden door. Wind still gusted occasionally, but they were able to scoop a bagful of snow into their plastic container. After securing the door again, Robyn and Katy carefully placed the snow-filled bag around Chaz's leg.

"Is there anything else we can do for now?" Danny asked.

"I don't think so. We'll have to wait out the storm before we can do anything else," Chaz answered. "But I think I promised you a story."

Danny threw another log on the fire and the kids gathered around Chaz. The fire's flickering light cast eerie shadows on the floor, and the howling wind sounded mournful.

"This had better be a happy story," Katy murmured.

Chaz smiled. "Well, most stories have good parts and bad parts," he said. "But what I'm about to tell you is all true—lots of it is a part of history.

"My family's history goes back to South Carolina. My great-great grandfather was Howell Davis. His family owned a cotton plantation, and life was good—until the Civil War broke out in 1861. Howell avoided joining the

Confederate Army, though he was a supporter. In 1863, when he was just seventeen years old, he left South Carolina against his parents' wishes, and moved to Montana. He was intrigued by the mountains and wide open spaces. He had quite a bit of money with him, and used it to purchase some land and buy cattle. Then, after the Civil War ended in 1865, he married a girl named Isabella. Because there was still a lot of tension among the states, and because Montana was in Union territory, he thought it would be wise to change his last name from Davis to King. He didn't want anyone to think he was related to the former Confederate President, Jefferson Davis.

"And about that time, he got caught up in the whole gold rush phenomenon. He did pretty good too. But then, his wife gave birth to my great-grandfather, Jefferson King in 1870, and Howell decided to stay at home and tend to the cattle.

"Jefferson took over the cattle ranch and also added wheat farming to increase the family's wealth. In 1890 he married a woman from back East. Her name was Priscilla. They had nine children—the last one, of which, was born in 1899 and who became my grandfather—William Charles King.

"William started a dairy farm and married my grandmother—Helen in 1914. Then in 1920 my father Isaac came along. He took over the dairy farming business when my grandfather was killed during a blizzard. He eventually married my mother—Elizabeth—on September 1, 1939, the very day the Germans invaded Poland—the beginning of World War II.

"Then, two years later, on December 6, 1941, I was born—the day before the Japanese attacked Pearl Harbor. My dad, along with countless other men, joined the army and went off to war, leaving behind a brand new baby and a young wife.

"Neighbors helped each other with harvesting, milking cows, and whatever else they had to do. My father was gone for the duration of the war. He ended up with the soldiers who landed on Normandy Beach in France, and was one of the first soldiers who marched into Germany.

"I was four years old when he came back. I'll never forget seeing him walk up the dirt road to our house. My mother was on the front porch watching for him. When she spotted him, she took off like a deer and ran into his arms. Then she turned toward me and waved for me to come. I was a little scared. After all, I didn't even know him. But when I saw his big smile and opened arms, I thought he was pretty cool."

Chaz stopped for a moment and stared out the window—even though nothing but the snowflakes that danced close to the window could be seen.

"So, how did you end up here in this shack?" Johnnie asked.

"Well, when I grew up I decided cattle ranching wasn't for me. In 1960, when I was just nineteen years old, I happened to see a film by a man called John Jay. He had been filming skiing events for a long time. Many said that the purpose of his documentaries was to give inspiration to the timid skiers and to make the bolder skiers even bolder.

"I was also in the second decade of what became known as the Golden Age of American Skiing. You see, the Europeans had claimed all the fame in skiing—especially in Norway, where alpine skiing originated. But Americans got caught up in the sport, and its popularity soared."

"Did you ever ski competitively?" Robyn asked.

"Yeah, I did enter a couple of winter competitions—did pretty good too, but I never pursued it," Chaz said.

"So, what did you do from the 1960s until now?" Johnnie asked.

Chaz took a deep breath. "Well, I got married for one thing, to a local girl named Diane. We had two boys, Charles, Jr. and Mark. When the kids came along, I went back to dairy farming in the summer, and ski patrolling in the winter."

"Wow! You were part of the ski patrol? Cool!" Johnnie said.

Chaz winced, and Johnnie wasn't sure if it was because Chaz's leg hurt or because of a bad memory. It was a while before he continued.

"My best friend Abe Bakker and I were both on ski patrol. We had taught our boys how to ski. He had two about the same age as mine.

"Then one day, a storm—much like the one tonight—struck quickly. My son Charlie and Abe's son Andrew were out on the slopes. It was getting really bad out, and the boys hadn't come in. So Abe and I put on our gear and headed out.

"We combed that mountainside—all the trails we

knew—but we couldn't find them. It was getting dark fast, and we knew we'd have to head back to the lodge.

"I didn't sleep at all that night. As soon as the sun came up the next morning, Abe, several other skiers and I took off. We yelled out their names all morning. Finally, shortly before noon, I heard someone calling. I yelled out for whoever it was to keep shouting out so I could follow the sound.

"I came to a steep cliff. There, clinging to a couple trees was my son Charlie. Farther down the cliff, crouched on a narrow ledge was Andrew. I hollered down to both of them and they looked up.

"I was so glad they were alive I cried. I had rope with me and a couple stakes. I hammered a stake into the ground, tied the rope around it and threw the other end down to Charlie. He knew what to do. He tied it around himself, kicked off his skis and held on.

"By this time, Abe and a couple other guys had caught up with me and helped hoist him up. Andrew was too far down for the rope to reach, but I got this idea that if I rappelled down to where Charlie had been with another rope tied around my waist, I could haul Andrew up.

"Abe helped me go over the edge. I reached the tree and straddled its base to keep myself from falling. Then I lowered the rope to Andrew. He tied it around his waist like I told him to, and then kicked off his skis. I was pulling and he was trying to climb up that slippery slope.

"My hands ached from gripping the rope, and my muscles were sore from pulling. It seemed I was doing all the work and Andrew wasn't climbing. I looked down and figured out right away what the problem was—he had broken his right leg and was trying to climb using only one.

"I yelled up to Abe and told him what the problem was. He instructed me to lower Andrew back onto the ledge and said they would get him up a different way. So I shouted to Andrew and carefully lowered him back down. When he landed on the ledge, his bad leg was under him. He jerked back and lost his balance."

Tears rolled down Chaz's face as he tried to choke out the rest of the story. "I tried with all my might to hang onto that rope. I nearly fell myself. My hands hurt so bad. My arms hurt. I could hear Abe yelling and screaming from above me. But I couldn't hold on. The weight of Andrew's body and the fact that he couldn't use both legs to climb back up made it impossible. The rope slipped out of my hands, and I watched helplessly as Andrew tumbled down to the bottom of the cliff.

"Andrew miraculously lived, but he was paralyzed from the waist down. I tried to visit—tried to talk to Abe, but he was too grief-stricken. Shortly thereafter, my wife Diane died of cancer. Both of my boys decided to leave Montana and live with relatives in Arizona. I sold the ranch and moved out here."

"My goodness!" Katy exclaimed. "You've been living out here for…"

"Since 1982," Chaz finished.

"I never knew what became of Andrew or his brother. And I don't know what became of Abe. Sure would love to see them again, though, and tell them how sorry I am—especially Abe. Maybe he could find it in his heart to forgive me."

Johnnie cocked his head to one side. "Abe Bakker," he thought to himself. "Now where have I heard that name before?"

CHAPTER 13

# Nighttime Surprises

The story seemed to wear out Chaz. He asked Danny if he would help him move away from the bed so he could lie down.

Katy placed the pillow under his head. "Can we do anything to make you more comfortable?" she asked.

He turned his face to her and smiled. "No, but thanks. You know, you kids are the only ones who I've told that story to. It felt kind of good to share it with someone. I'm feeling tired. Think I'll take a nap. There are a couple more blankets around here somewhere. Help yourself—and take some more soup, if you want."

It didn't take long for Chaz to fall asleep. Johnnie scooted closer to the fire and stared at the dancing flames. Robyn found three blankets. She and Katy decided to share one, and gave the others to Danny and

Johnnie.

Danny peered out the window. Both windows rattled as the wind blew against them. The storm grew stronger, and Danny felt the cold air force itself through the cracks in the wood. A strong gust of wind struck the cabin, and the walls creaked in response.

"We'd better put another big log or two on the fire," Danny said. "I hope our parents aren't too worried about us. I wonder what they're doing right now."

"Mom's probably having a panic attack," Katy said. "I can't wait until we get back home—I just hope we don't get in too much trouble. We never should have come so far into these woods."

"Well, we shouldn't worry about it now," Johnnie said. "We need to focus on keeping warm and making sure our friend, here, is okay."

Johnnie looked over at Chaz who lay shivering under the blankets. His face was pale. "I'm worried about him. It looks like he has a fever."

"Look!" cried Katy. She pointed at a blood stain seeping through the blanket that covered Chaz.

Danny quickly uncovered Chaz's leg. "Oh no," he groaned. "Looks like he cut his leg—maybe when he fell.

It doesn't look like he's bleeding a lot. What should we do?"

"Find a knife," Katy said.

"What!?" Johnnie exclaimed. "Are you thinking of doing surgery or something crazy like that?"

Katy rolled her eyes and stood with her hands on her hips. "Get real!" she said. "I'm just going to cut away part of his pants leg so we can see how badly he's hurt, and clean the wound."

"Oh!" Johnnie said, clearly relieved.

Robyn brought over a knife and put the blade in the fire. "This will kill the germs," she said. "I saw this in a movie once."

Then she handed the knife to Katy who carefully cut away some of the blood-stained fabric.

"Wow! He's got a bad cut on his leg, and look at his ankle," Danny said.

"It looks weird," Katy said.

Robyn looked at it and said, "I think it's broken. What if we put some snow in one of his pots and heat it up a bit. We could use the warm water to clean the cut. Look around for some gauze or some clean cloth so we can wrap it and stop the bleeding."

"We need to get him to a hospital as soon as possible," Johnnie said.

"I agree," Danny said. "But until this storm stops, we're stuck."

The kids cleaned the open wound the best they could. Robyn had found some cloth handkerchiefs. She and Katy tied them together to form a bandage.

Chaz stirred and opened his eyes slightly. "Thanks," he barely whispered. Then he closed his eyes again.

"There's nothing more we can do tonight. We should all try to get some sleep," Johnnie said, suddenly realizing how tired he was.

Robyn yawned. "I agree." She wrapped herself up in the blanket.

"Hey! That blanket's for both of us," Katy cried.

Robyn smiled and said, "Well then, you'd better get over here quick and claim your half before I take it all!"

The two girls lay near the fire and snuggled under the blanket.

Johnnie hugged his blanket around him, as he curled up on the wooden floor. He rolled up his jacket and used it as a pillow. The room felt warm, and soon Johnnie felt himself drift off to a dreamless sleep.

* * *

It seemed like only a few minutes later when Johnnie was awakened by a shrill scream. "Help!" Robyn shrieked. "A bear! A giant bear!"

The entire cabin filled with sounds of panic, as Johnnie, Katy and Danny scrambled to find the flashlight. The fire had died down—just a dim glow from some of the embers provided all the available light.

Johnnie could barely make out Robyn's silhouette at the far side of the cabin.

"I heard something scratching so I got up to investigate, and then....Look! Look!" It's still there!" Robyn yelled.

Finally Danny located the flashlight and clicked it on. Johnnie, Katy and Danny stared at Robyn, and then looked at each other. They erupted in laughter.

There, standing at what she must have thought was a window, was Robyn—looking at a disheveled image of herself in a mirror that hung on the wall.

When Robyn realized what had happened, she slumped down on the floor, her hand over her heart. "It's not funny!" she said meekly. But her mouth couldn't help but twist upward into a grin. She started to laugh.

"I guess that was pretty funny," she admitted.

A low moan from Chaz quieted the kids instantly.

"It's still pitch dark outside," Johnnie noted. "Let's throw another log on the fire and get some sleep."

It was hard for Johnnie to settle back down, but eventually he drifted off to a restless sleep. He tossed and turned on the hard floor. Gradually he was awakened by noises that seemed far off at first, but that grew louder as he became more awake.

"Something's moving outside," he murmured to himself. It was hard to distinguish the sound over the howling wind.

"Aw, it's just my imagination," Johnnie said softly. "I'm probably still spooked by that whole Robyn scene." He chuckled lightly as he remembered the look on Robyn's face when she saw herself in the mirror.

But then the noise became more distinct. Johnnie could hear a definite crunching sound, as if something or someone was walking in the snow.

Cautiously, Johnnie pulled his body up to the door so he could hear it better. He placed his ear next to a crack and listened. Just then, the door shook violently, as if something had struck it from the other side. He jumped back, but nothing happened. Slowly, he scooted toward the door again and listened. He could hear the frantic sniffing and scratching of some type of animal.

Johnnie drew back in horror as a deep growl rumbled through the crack.

"What is it Johnnie?" Robyn whispered. She sat looking at him from across the room.

"I-I don't know!" Johnnie whispered back. "Whatever is out there, nearly broke through the door."

Robyn and Johnnie stayed still. Johnnie held his breath. "I don't hear it anymore," Johnnie said softly. "I think it's gone."

"Should we wake up the others?" Robyn asked.

"No, we're safe in here. Let them sleep," Johnnie answered. "We've had enough excitement for one night."

He smiled weakly at Robyn, who raised an eyebrow at him.

"Just kidding," Johnnie said.

With that, the two curled up under their blankets and fell uneasily back to sleep.

CHAPTER 14

# Survival

"Johnnie! Wake up!"

Johnnie felt someone nudge him.

"Huh? Where am I?" Johnnie murmured.

"In Chaz's cabin—remember?" Johnnie turned and saw Danny kneeling beside him. He rubbed his eyes and looked around. The room was dimly lit, and the fire had died down to just a few glowing embers.

"There's just a few more logs," Danny whispered. "I'm going to put one of them on now, but we've got to get more somehow. It's still storming outside, and if the fire dies we'll all freeze to death."

Katy and Robyn stirred. "What's going on?" Robyn whispered.

"It's okay," Danny said. "I'm going outside to see if there's some more firewood near the cabin."

Danny pulled on his boots and zipped his jacket. He looked out the window. "It sure looks cold out there, and I can hardly see a thing through all that blowing snow. I won't stay out there too long."

Danny unbarred the door and pushed hard to open it against the snow that had piled up against it. After much effort, he managed to open the door wide enough to slip through. Wind and snow rushed at him as if it had been waiting on the doorstep to come whirling inside. He pushed the door shut again once he was outside.

Johnnie inched toward the door and waited. A few minutes later, Danny pulled the door open again and stepped inside. He shut it and slumped down on the floor next to Johnnie. Though he had been outside for just a few minutes, snow covered his jacket.

"No luck," Danny said. "I couldn't see a thing with all the blowing snow. The fire hasn't died just yet, and we still have one more log. We should be okay for awhile, but we'll need to find more wood soon."

Chaz moaned from the other side of the room. Katy

went over to him and lay her hand on his forehead. "He's burning up! Quick, somebody get a cloth and scrape some of the snow off Danny's jacket into it."

Robyn located a dish rag and filled it with the snow. She folded it in thirds to keep the snow inside. Then she handed it to Katy, who placed it carefully over Chaz's forehead.

Hours passed and the wind began to die down. Johnnie pulled himself up onto a chair by the window. He saw huge flakes gently drift toward the earth.

"Hey!" he said, brightening. "The storm has let up! Looks like the sky is getting patches of blue. I'm sure someone will find us soon. Or maybe we can use the snowmobiles to head back into town so we can get some help!"

Danny opened the front door again and stepped outside. He came back in looking glum. "I don't think we'll be going anywhere on snowmobiles," he announced. "They are completely covered by a snow drift that's got to be ten feet high!"

"Well, maybe we could walk," Robyn said.

"Walk?" Katy looked out the window. "This snow looks higher than our heads in some places. I wonder how far it is back to town."

Danny thought a moment. "It took us about an hour and a half to reach this place on snowmobiles. At times we were going about twenty miles per hour, so I'd say the town is at least twenty miles away."

"Twenty miles!" Robyn cried. "We'd never make it in all this snow. The fastest we could go would be about two miles an hour. We're talking ten hours of steady walking!"

"Well, for sure, *I'm* not walking out of here," Johnnie said.

"Maybe we should go back and look for Dad's cell phone," Katy suggested.

"Katy, we looked and looked for that thing *before* the storm hit," reminded Danny. "What are our chances of finding it now?"

"I don't know, I just feel like we should do *something*," she said. Her eyes filled with tears.

"I'd better go out again and try to get some more wood," Danny said. "I think I remember seeing a woodpile underneath a tarp on the side of the house. It's probably buried now, but maybe not too deeply. It was piled on the side of the house facing away from the wind."

"Good idea," said Johnnie. "But be careful out there. Later last night, after Robyn's bear scare, we both woke up and heard some kind of animal. Whatever it was, it sure sounded mean."

"I doubt seriously that it was a bear," Danny said. "Bears hibernate. It was probably just a raccoon or some kind of rodent seeking shelter from the storm."

Johnnie felt doubtful but didn't say anything more. He watched Danny open the door and go outside. He noticed patches of sunlight on the cabin's floor. The storm was definitely over. He felt sure that someone would rescue them.

"I'd better look for something to eat," said Robyn. She rummaged through the kitchen and came up with two cans of split pea soup. "We can add this to what's left of the chicken noodle soup."

"Anything sounds good," Katy said. "I'm hungry!"

After adding the ingredients to the pot, the girls sat near Chaz, keeping an eye on him. Johnnie tried to relax, but the sounds he and Robyn had heard the night before, sounded more ferocious than a raccoon or mouse.

"Hey! I wonder where Danny is?" Katy said. "He's

been out there for a long time."

Johnnie pulled himself up to the chair next to the window and looked out.

"Oh no!" he yelled. "Danny!"

Katy and Robyn scurried to the window. "Over there!" Johnnie pointed.

Katy screamed.

Standing on top of a snow drift, just twenty feet from the cabin, a mountain lion crouched, its eyes fixed on Danny, who stood as if frozen—a bundle of logs in his arms.

Johnnie noted that the animal wore a scar from the top of its head, down across its nose. Its ribs could be clearly seen through its light tan-colored coat. Johnnie saw the mountain lion crouch a little lower.

"It's going to pounce!" Johnnie yelled. Katy screamed even louder and began pounding on the window. Robyn ran and grabbed a pan and banged it against the wall, attempting to scare the lion away.

The mountain lion suddenly turned and ran off back into the woods. Katy ran to the front door and quickly opened it. Danny jumped inside and landed on his stomach, on top of all the logs he had been carrying.

Katy pulled the door shut, as Robyn and Johnnie hurried to find out if Danny was okay.

"That must have been the animal Robyn and I heard last night," Johnnie said.

Danny just leaned against one of the cabin walls without saying a word. The girls quickly retrieved the logs, and Johnnie pulled himself next to his friend.

"You sure you're all right?" he asked.

Danny nodded. Then he drew in a deep breath. "I thought I was a goner for sure," he said.

The hours passed. Chaz awoke a few times and muttered something, but Johnnie couldn't understand anything he said. Exhausted, Chaz closed his eyes once more.

After Danny's close call with the mountain lion, the kids decided to stay in the cabin. "We could play 'I Spy'," Katie suggested.

Johnnie looked out the window and said, "Well, *I* spy something white!"

They all laughed. The kids tried to keep busy by making up games, but the afternoon dragged by. Soon Johnnie could see the long shadows of the trees stretch out over the mounds of snow as the sun began to set behind the mountains.

"Do you think that mountain lion is still out there?" Robyn asked.

"After the way Katy screamed and banged on the window, I doubt we'll see that stupid mountain lion again," Johnnie said. "He's probably on his way to Canada by now!"

Katy blushed. "Hey! Chaz needs more snow for his leg," she said, obviously trying to take the attention off herself.

"Danny, can you hold the door open so I can scoop some more snow into the bag?"

"Sure," he said. "But go fast. I don't want any more run-ins with that mountain lion."

After filling the bag with snow, she also replenished the snow in the dish rag and put it back on Chaz's head. "He looks worse and worse with each hour," Katy commented.

"Now that the storm is over, our parents will start looking for us, for sure," Johnnie said. "I'll bet there are rescue teams already out searching, and when they find us, they can rush Chaz to a hospital."

Suddenly Johnnie's stomach growled. "I don't know

about you guys, but I'm hungry.

"There's some of the chicken noodle soup left," Robyn said. "And I saw a few cans of green beans on the counter."

"Tell you what," Danny said. "Johnnie and I will scout around for *something* besides soup and green beans while you two look after Chaz."

"Deal!" Robyn agreed. "Just hurry! I'm starving."

After searching through the kitchen, Danny and Johnnie discovered a can of tuna fish, some canned peas and corn and a box of macaroni and cheese.

"Hey! Can you make macaroni and cheese without milk?" Danny asked.

"There's some powdered milk on the shelf," Johnnie said. "We could use that."

"Great! Let's mix the tuna fish, corn and peas with the macaroni and cheese. It'll be awesome."

When dinner was ready, both girls looked suspiciously at the boys' creation, but hunger overtook caution.

"Should we try to wake up Chaz?" Johnnie asked.

Katy shook the old man gently. "Chaz. Chaz!" she said. "Do you want some tuna stuff?"

Chaz moved slightly and through heavy eyelids, looked at Katy. Finally, he shook his head and closed his eyes again.

"I'm worried about him," Katy said.

"As long as we keep this fire going, the smoke might alert rescue workers as to where we are," Johnnie said. "And the sooner they get here, the sooner Chaz can get some help."

"I hope someone sees the smoke in the chimney soon," Danny said. "But it's dark now, and I doubt that anyone will see it tonight."

"Let's throw a couple more logs on the fire and try to get some rest," Johnnie suggested. "It's been a long day for all of us."

They huddled near the fire and tried to take their minds off their predicament by telling stories and jokes. Occasionally, Katy or Robyn would check on Chaz. They put fresh snow in the bag for his leg and in the dish rag for his forehead one last time before they settled down for the second night.

One by one, each fell asleep. Johnnie was the last one. He listened intently for "crunching" sounds in the snow, but the woods were silent. Eventually, he drifted off to sleep.

* * *

The next morning, Johnnie awoke to a faint humming sound. Danny's eyes popped open too. Danny glanced at his watch.

"It's nine o'clock," he shouted. "Time to get up. I hear something!"

Johnnie glanced out the window. A sunny day greeted him. He quickly helped gather the logs and put them in the fireplace. The humming noise grew louder.

"It's an airplane!" Danny shouted.

Johnnie cheered. "Finally! We're going to get rescued."

They ran out to see if they could spot the plane. Johnnie waited near the front door. The air was clear and brisk.

"See anything?" he yelled.

The kids came running back into the cabin, shivering. "No, it's too far away yet," Danny said.

They closed the door and looked over at Chaz, who was still unconscious. Katy sat next to him and patted his shoulder. "It won't be much longer, Chaz. The airplane is coming. They'll find us. I just know it!"

About ten minutes later, they heard the airplane pass directly over them. "I'm sure they've spotted the cabin," Johnnie said.

But a half hour passed, and nothing more was heard. "I've just got to get out of this cabin," Johnnie suddenly announced. "I've been stuck in here for nearly three days. I'm going to go outside and see if I can hear any more planes."

"What about that mountain lion?" asked Danny.

"It's been almost a whole day since we've seen or heard that pitiful creature. I'm sure he's long gone."

"Yeah, I suppose you're right. Go ahead. But stay near the cabin," Danny said. "I'll keep the fire going."
Johnnie slipped on his jacket and boots. "I just want to sit outside in the snow awhile," he explained. "The fresh air will feel good."

"Go for it!" Robyn said, and she smiled at him. She held the door open and Johnnie slid out into the snow. It had been somewhat packed down by Danny's footprints the day before.

Johnnie squinted as he looked up into the clear blue sky. The air was crisp but the sun felt warm through his jacket. He watched his breath make swirls of steam. He closed his eyes to enjoy the mixture of cold and warm sensations.

*Crunch.* Johnnie's eyes popped open. The sound was too familiar. He scanned the area and saw nothing out of place, at first. But then suddenly, in the deep shadows of the pine forest, he saw the mountain lion. It quietly leapt onto the snow drift just ten feet in front of him. Its yellow eyes narrowed as it regarded Johnnie.

Panic settled in. Johnnie was so afraid, he couldn't utter a sound. The big cat ventured closer, crouching as it walked.

Johnnie shook himself free of his fear. He grabbed a fistful of snow and wadded it into the hardest snowball he could. As the lion crept closer, Johnnie threw the snowball as hard as he could.

Smack! Right on target, the snowball hit the cat in the head. Instead of running away, however, the lion bared its teeth and crouched, ready to pounce.

Finally, Johnnie found his voice. "HELP! GET BACK! SOMEBODY HELP ME!"

The next thing Johnnie knew, the lion had pounced and was in the air coming right at him. It seemed like everything was happening in slow motion. The lion's claws extended, it's mouth opened, fangs ready to rip his flesh apart. And then—blackness.

CHAPTER 15

# The Christmas Gift

The room was dark at first, until his vision began to return. Johnnie saw blurry figures standing on either side of him.

"He's coming to," he heard his mother say.

Blinking, Johnnie tried to clear his head. Things began to come into focus. Johnnie looked around and saw his parents' worried faces.

"Where am I? What happened?" Johnnie asked, still in a daze.

"You're at the hospital," Mr. Jacobson said.

"The mountain lion…" Johnnie began.

"A rescue worker came up over the ridge and spotted it. Fortunately, for all of us, he shot the lion as it leapt in midair."

"Am I okay?" Johnnie said, remembering the menacing look on the lion's face.

"You're just fine. The rescue workers wanted to bring you into the hospital so the doctors could check you over. The doc says that once you're able to sit up on your own, we can take you out of here."

"I remember seeing the lion jump—and then everything went dark," Johnnie said.

"When the lion jumped, you fell sideways and hit your head," Johnnie's mother explained. "It knocked you out."

"What about Chaz and the others?" Johnnie asked. "Are they okay?"

"Danny, Katy and Robyn are all just fine," his father reassured him. "Chaz was lifted out by helicopter and taken to the hospital in Billings. He's in serious but stable condition with an infected leg. The doctors there assured us that he would be okay."

Soon Johnnie was able to sit up, and the doctor released him from the hospital. As he arrived in the emergency room lobby, he saw his friends waiting anxiously for him. When they spotted Johnnie, they ran up to him and hugged him. Together, they headed outside to await the van that would take them back to the inn.

Everyone thanked the rescue workers over and over, offering to buy them dinner or do something to show their appreciation.

"No need for that," one of the workers said. "Our reward is a successful rescue."

"Could you please call us and let us know how Chaz is?" Johnnie asked.

"Sure thing," the worker said.

Once inside the guest cabin, the kids stumbled over each other's words, trying to tell their families what happened.

Johnnie relayed Chaz's story about losing his grip on the rope and watching Andrew fall. He said, "I wish there was something we could do for him. He seems so lonely."

"Let's all think about it on our way back to Red Lodge," Mr. Jacobson said.

"What!? We're leaving already?" Katy asked.

Mrs. Randall stroked her daughter's hair. "Yes, I'm afraid today is check-out day."

"But what about the snowmobiles back at Chaz's cabin?" Johnnie asked.

"The rescue workers said they'd dig out the snowmobiles and return them," Mr. Anderson replied. "Under the circumstances, the rental office said they wouldn't charge us extra as long as the snowmobiles were returned."

* * *

During the long ride back to Red Lodge, Johnnie kept mulling over Chaz's story. But by the time they were halfway back, he felt himself nodding off to sleep. When the van stopped in front of the inn, Johnnie awoke.

It didn't take much coaxing to get Johnnie, Danny, Katy and Robyn to take their showers and get into bed. Johnnie couldn't remember when a nice warm, soft bed ever felt so good.

The next morning, after breakfast, Johnnie could hardly wait to get up to the ski lodge. "Anxious for some skiing?" his father asked.

"Actually, I'm anxious about something else," he said. "But I have to do some investigating first."

Just then Mr. Jacobson's phone chirped. He flipped it open and said, "Hello? Oh yes! He is? Okay, I'll tell them. Thank you!"

Johnnie's eyes widened. "Was that the rescue worker?"

"Yes," Mr. Jacobson answered. "Chaz is resting comfortably in the hospital. He suffered a badly broken ankle, and the cut had become infected. But they've got him on some antibiotics, and the worker said he'll be fine."

Johnnie breathed a sigh of relief. "Can we go see him?" he asked.

"Since tomorrow's Christmas, I suppose we can travel over to Billings, if the others agree," Mr. Jacobson said.

Once they all arrived at the lodge, Mr. Jacobson told the others about Chaz and Johnnie's desire to visit him. They all agreed that would be a good idea.

"There's something else I want to look into," Johnnie said, as he wheeled himself into the large hall of the lodge.

Danny, Katy and Robyn followed. "What's up?" Danny asked.

"You guys wait here," Johnnie said. "If this all checks out, I'll let you in on it."

They all started to protest, but when Danny saw Johnnie's determined look, he said, "Oh, okay. Let him go. Meanwhile, let's get our ski gear on and enjoy the slopes."

A little while later, Johnnie joined the others on the ski slope. Gary, his ski instructor met him and escorted him to the chair lift. "I hear you've had quite the adventure," Gary said. "With an adventuresome spirit like that, you won't need me to escort you down the hill—will you?"

Johnnie looked uncertain. "Tell you what," Johnnie said. "You ski down first and then watch me."

"Deal!" Gary said.

Johnnie watched Gary swish and glide all the way to the bottom, then turn to wait for Johnnie.

"Ho boy!" Johnnie said. "How do I get myself into these situations?"

With that, he took a deep breath and pushed off. He remembered all the instructions Gary had given him, about using his upper body to make the curves. The wind in his face and the sheer speed felt exhilarating. He laughed with pure joy as he neared the bottom. Gary stood there and applauded as Johnnie came to a halt.

"Great job! Johnnie. If you keep that up, you just might make it to the Paralympics some day!"

Johnnie made a few more runs down the slope, and only wiped out twice before it was time to come back to the lodge. Danny, Katy and Robyn were anxiously waiting for him.

"Well?" Katy asked. "Are we going to find out what's going on or not?"

Johnnie rubbed his chin thoughtfully. "Maybe," he teased. Then he smiled. "You are never going to believe the Christmas present I have for Chaz!"

The kids huddled around a big, round wooden table while Johnnie told them all about it. "I told my dad too," he said. "And he thinks it's a great idea!"

\* \* \*

Johnnie awoke early on Christmas morning. The stars were still twinkling in the sky and a thin line of light peeked over the eastern horizon.

"Merry Christmas!" he shouted.

He heard his dad groan, "What time is it?"

"It's time to get up! It's Christmas morning!" Johnnie yelled. "Dibs on the shower."

He transferred into his wheelchair and rolled into the bathroom. Soon the warm water cascaded over his hair and onto his body. The water felt great on his sore muscles from his day of skiing. But it was a good sore. Johnnie beamed with joy. What a day this was going to be.

Because it was Christmas, all the restaurants were closed, but the families had prepared ahead of time. They had purchased donuts, juice and coffee at the local store, and just ate in their rooms. By 6:30 that morning, the Randalls, Andersons and Jacobsons gathered together in the parking lot.

"Now we have to go back to the ski lodge to pick up 'the package'," Johnnie said.

"You're sure it will be ready?" Mrs. Jacobson asked.

"Oh, I'm sure!"

\* \* \*

The ride over to Billings took about six hours, and then it took another twenty minutes to find the hospital. Fortunately, Mrs. Jacobson had thought to pack a lunch so they wouldn't have to stop to eat.

Just around one o'clock, everyone piled out of the vans and hurried into the hospital lobby. At the information desk, Mr. Jacobson asked where Chaz King's room was.

The receptionist looked up and eyed all of them. "It's a little early for visitors," she said.

"But it's Christmas," Johnnie insisted. "And we've

brought him a special Christmas present."

The receptionist peered over the desk and down at Johnnie. She raised an eyebrow, and then smiled. "You are absolutely right. It *is* Christmas. If you can all be quiet as mice, take the elevator to the second floor. He's in room 211."

Everyone piled into the elevator. Johnnie shook with excitement as they rode up to the second floor. Slowly they made their way down the shiny linoleum hallway and stopped outside of Chaz's room.

"Let's let the kids go in first, and make sure he's up to visitors," Mr. Anderson suggested.

Johnnie wheeled in first, followed by Robyn, Katy and Danny. Chaz's face was turned toward the window. Johnnie wheeled up beside the bed. "Chaz?" he whispered. "Are you awake?"

Chaz turned his head and stared. "I can't believe it!" he said. "You came to visit me!"

"Merry Christmas!" they all said together.

Johnnie said, "We heard that you broke your ankle in a couple places but that you'll be all right."

"That's what they tell me," Chaz said. "But I don't know where I'm going to go when they release me from here. It's too hard to get back to my place on two good legs, let alone one good and one bad.  Even with a snowmobile, I don't think I'd make it."

Johnnie grinned. "Well, we have brought you a Christmas present that might help," he said.

"What? A present? For me?" Chaz's eyes misted. "I haven't had a Christmas present in years!"

Johnnie turned his chair around. "I'll just go out in the hallway and get it," he said. "Close your eyes until I tell you to open them."

A few minutes later, Johnnie wheeled next to Chaz's bed. "Okay," he said. "Open your eyes!"

Chaz's eyes flew open. He stared at all the adults in the room. Then he fixed his eyes on one person—someone who looked vaguely familiar.

"Merry Christmas, Chaz," Abraham Bakker said.

"Abe? Is that really you?" Chaz choked up.

"Sure is," Abe said as he moved closer to Chaz's bedside. "I have wondered for years whatever became of you. And here you are—in a hospital bed with a banged-up ankle."

"I could never face you after what happened to Andrew. You seemed so angry—so hurt," Chaz said.

"And I knew it was all my fault. I just didn't know what to do. And then Diane died and my kids moved away, and—well, I figured I should just move away too."

Abe got down on his knees and held Chaz's hand. "Forgive me, my friend. I did blame you at first, and I just couldn't talk about it. But one day I realized that you had done everything a human being could have done. It was just one of those things—an accident.

"As for Andrew, well being a paraplegic was the beginning of a whole new, wonderful life for him! It took awhile, but he learned how to ski and participate in other wheelchair sports.

"In fact, he and his teammates are in Utah training for the Winter Paralympics. Andrew specializes in the Men's Downhill event."

Chaz's eyes widened and his mouth dropped open. "Andrew is skiing again? And he's still in a wheelchair?"

Abe chuckled. "You've been away too long! A lot has happened to make wheelchairs, bicycles, skis—all sorts of equipment, available to people with all kinds of disabilities."

Abe stood up and smiled. "I can't tell you how grateful I am that these kids found you," he said.

Chaz reached over and clasped his friend's hand. "All these years, I've been wanting to ask you for your forgiveness, and now you ask me for mine. When I was down in that ravine with my broken ankle, I thought about Andrew. I thought that maybe God was getting me back. But then these four kids came along and risked their lives to save mine."

"Well, for now, it looks like it's just you and me," Abe said. "My wife died a few years back, and my other son is in California with his wife and kids. Andrew will be back in the spring—and I know he's going to be happy to see you. Say, do you think two old, best friends could live over in Red Lodge? I hear that the ski lodge could use some expert advice on fitting people properly with skis and such. The pay's decent and the food is good. There's always time to play some checkers or just enjoy a good movie. Plus, I want you to see what folks with disabilities can do. It's amazing!"

Chaz's lower lip trembled, and he wiped his eyes. "I think I'd like that," he said. Then he looked at Johnnie and the kids. "This is the best Christmas present I ever got!"

He looked at the parents all standing there—not a

dry eye in the place. "You have raised yourselves some mighty fine kids, and you are to be congratulated. Anytime you want to come back and visit, you are more than welcome."

"And that goes double for me," Abe chimed in.

\* \* \*

As everyone headed back to Michigan on the plane, Johnnie turned a piece of the pink Montana rock over and over in his hand. Danny leaned over and said, "Nick's going to love that rock. He can add it to his collection!"

"Yeah, but he is going to go nuts when he finds out the adventure he missed," Johnnie said with a grin.

# Alternatives in Motion

A portion of the proceeds from sales of The Gun Lake Adventure Series goes to support the nonprofit organization Alternatives in Motion, founded by Johnnie Tuitel in 1995. The mission of Alternatives in Motion is to provide wheelchairs to individuals who do not qualify for other assistance and who could not obtain such equipment without financial aid.

For further information or to make a donation, please contact Johnnie Tuitel at:

Alternatives in Motion
1916 Breton Rd., SE
Grand Rapids, MI 49506
616.493.2620 (voice)
616.493.2621 (fax)
www.alternativesinmotion.org

Alternatives in Motion is a nonprofit 501(c)(3) organization.

# Gun Lake
## Adventure Series

**From the Children's Bookwatch—Midwest Book Review:**

"The fourth in Cedar Tree Publishing's outstanding "Gun Lake Adventure" series, *Searching the Noonday Trail* is another great novel by Johnnie Tuitel and Sharon Lamson for young readers which is wonderfully written and totally entertaining from first page to last."

**From Early On Michigan Newsletter:**

"This little book is a gem."

**From Pooh's Corner Bookstore:**

"The Gun Lake Adventure Series provides action, adventure, fun and friends...elements kids love to read about."

**From the Grand Rapids Press:**

"...(the) Gun Lake Adventure Series is capturing the attention of young readers in Grand Rapids and beyond."

**From the Children's Bookwatch—Midwest Book Review:**

"...A pure delight for young readers, *Discovery on Blackbird Island* is the third volume in the 'Gun Lake Adventure Series,' and like its predecessors, *The Barn at Gun Lake* and *Mystery Explosion!*, showcase the substantial storytelling talents of Johnnie Tuitel and Sharon Lamson.

## The Gun Lake Adventure Series
## by Johnnie Tuitel and Sharon Lamson

**The Barn at Gun Lake** (1998, Cedar Tree Publishing, $5.99 paperback, **Book 1**)
The Gun Lake kids stumble upon some modern pirates when they find an illegal copy of popular CDs in a deserted barn. While solving the mystery, there is a boat chase and then a dangerous wheelchair chase through the woods.

**Mystery Explosion!** (1999, Cedar Tree Publishing, $5.99 paperback, **Book 2**)
First there is an explosion. Then an arrest is made that shocks the quiet town of Gun Lake. A stranger in town and a search for his identity paves the way for another fast-paced mystery. Friendship and loyalties are tested as Johnnie Jacobson and his friends try to find the answers to "Who did it?" and "Why?"

**Discovery on Blackbird Island** (2000, Cedar Tree Publishing, $5.99 paperback, **Book 3**)
Blackbird Island—a small, quiet uninhabited island in Gun Lake. Or is it? A disturbing discovery sends Johnnie Jacobson and his friends on yet another Gun Lake adventure filled with schemes, action and mysteries to solve.

**Searching the Noonday Trail** (2000, Cedar Tree Publishing, $5.99 paperback, **Book 4**)

Summer's over and Johnnie is nervous about going to a new school. Will it be as adventuresome as the summer was? Johnnie's not too sure. But a secret football play and a field trip to where Chief Noonday and the Ottawa tribe used to live put Johnnie and his Gun Lake friends hot on the trail of another exciting adventure.

# About the Authors:

*Johnnie Tuitel,* who has cerebral palsy and uses a wheelchair, is a noted speaker nationally. Through his company Tap Shoe Productions, he talks to students, business people and community organizations. His humor and real-life stories help people understand what life with a disability is like. Johnnie and his wife Deb, and their three sons live in Grand Rapids, Michigan.

*Sharon Lamson* is a free-lance writer who is familiar with disability issues. She has been published with Tommy Nelson Publishers *(Wild and Wacky But Totally True Bible Stories*—both storybook and audio scripts) and Zondervan Publishing (leader's and participant's guides for Dave and Claudia Arp's *Second Half of Marriage* and the leader's and participant's guides for Drs. Les and Leslie Parrott's *Relationships).* Sharon and her husband Robert live in Norton Shores, Michigan. They have four soon-to-be-out-of-the-nest children.